The Story
of a
Long-Distance
Marriage

Siddhesh Inamdar is a writer and editor.

He studied English Literature at St Xavier's College, Mumbai, and Delhi University, and journalism at the Asian College of Journalism, Chennai. He worked with *The Hindu*, *DNA* and *Hindustan Times* and is now in publishing. He lives in Delhi with his wife, daughter and three cats.

The

Story of

a

Long-Distance

Marriage

SIDDHESH INAMDAR

HarperCollins *Publishers* India

First published in India by
HarperCollins *Publishers* in 2018
A-75, Sector 57, Noida, Uttar Pradesh 201301, India
www.harpercollins.co.in

2 4 6 8 10 9 7 5 3 1

P-ISBN: 978-93-5277-589-7
E-ISBN: 978-93-5277-590-3

This is a work of fiction and all characters and incidents described in this book are the product of the author's imagination. Any resemblance to actual persons, living or dead, is entirely coincidental.

Siddhesh Inamdar asserts the moral right
to be identified as the author of this work.

Typeset in 11/14.1 Sabon LT Std
Manipal Digital Systems, Manipal

Printed and bound at
Thomson Press (India) Ltd

*For
Blessy*

Contents

Ira

Distance

Love

Contents

Love is an institution of revolution;
in it you create new worlds.

Antonio Negri and Michael Hardt

Ira

Travel is flight and pursuit in equal parts.
Paul Theroux

1
Departure

Ira is leaving.

The realization hits me straight in the guts, as if out of nowhere, even though I have known for two months that this was coming. The smile I had kept on my face all day fades now at midnight and I sit. She is too busy to notice. She checks if her ticket is in her handbag along with the passport. She is a blur as she rushes from one room to another, ticking off items on her list. In the bedroom, she zips the last of her suitcases shut and then wheels it to the drawing room, leaving it standing near the door with a sense of finality.

From the balcony of our barsati, she gets her floral-patterned bathrobe that has been left to dry on the clothesline. Finally, she goes into the bathroom and closes the door. There is silence for a few seconds, during which she undresses, and then I hear the sound of water erupting from the showerhead, slowing her instantly,

3

and I am left staring at the door. I look at her clothes laid out on the bed: a full-sleeve red-and-blue check shirt, beige corduroys and her JNU sweater—too warm for the August heat in Delhi but just right for where she is about to go. Their limp, empty limbs make me feel like she is leaving my life forever. Like I will wake up tomorrow and realize I have no memory of her.

I think of the body that will fill those clothes as soon as she is out of the bathroom. I think of her standing under the shower, tying her hair on top of her head in a bun, closing her eyes and looking calm and perfectly in control. I think of the water sliding down her body. I have been in denial for weeks, but now it takes me no time to admit to myself that this is it. This is finally happening. Ira *is* leaving.

*

It all began in May, when she heard back from the dean of the Department of Art History at a prestigious institute in New York. He had loved and accepted her application for their master's programme. We went to Bombay for our first wedding anniversary, in June. That day she had to appear for an interview for a scholarship. The amount would have covered her tuition fees and living expenses for two years. But she did not make the cut. She spent our first anniversary heartbroken.

She wrote to the dean, saying she wouldn't be able to accept the offer after all. At twenty-seven, both of us were just a couple of years into our low-paying jobs. There was no way we could afford to pay the fees on our own, or even take a loan while I continued to pay rent in Delhi. She was upset that entire month. Studying in New York had been her dream.

And then some time towards the end of July I was at work when she called me. The dean had written to her again, offering a full fee waiver, leaving us to take just a small loan for her living expenses. There was no way she was going to say no to an offer as good as that. The loan, the visa, the goodbye—everything rolled quickly after that.

And today, within a month of that second email, Ira is all set to fly.

*

I step out on the balcony. Three floors below, the road circling the DDA flats of Shahpur Jat is almost empty. There is only the packed row of parked cars and a vegetable vendor having dinner with his wife under a gasoline lamp on his cart. Towering over them are the dark tops of wide-canopied trees in the Asian Games Village across the road—a view we had fallen in love with when we had first come to see the house. I don't know whether it is the idea of Ira under the shower, the sight of her clothes on the bed, the couple sharing a meal, or the memory of us standing in the balcony and watching the sun set at the end of a long and tiring day of house hunting—but I cave and start crying like a child.

The landlord, who lives on the first floor, must surely have heard me over the laughter of *Comedy Nights* and wondered if Ira and I are fighting. Sunil is a middle-aged, middle-class guy from UP, with a Honda CRV, a teenage son and daughter, and a beautiful, much younger-looking wife. She will also surely come upstairs to offer prasad from the temple in the back lane and whisper a word of advice about keeping marital discord within the four solid walls of the house they have built instead of taking it out on to the balcony where the neighbours can hear. But I still stay there for a long time.

'Rohan,' I hear Ira call out from inside the house, 'are you crying? Come back in.'

I don't want to oblige but I turn around and see her in her bathrobe. She hugs me as soon as I step in. There is the whiff of almond oil in her hair and a little sweat on the back of her neck—things that take me back to every time my face has rested against her bare shoulders.

'Why are you crying?' she asks.

'What do you think?'

'We talked about this, didn't we?' She almost sounds maternal, which she rarely does.

'Yes, I know,' I say. 'That's what I've been telling myself the whole day. You're only going away for a year; we can Skype every day; it's an opportunity of a lifetime; you always wanted to study in New York. But I can't do it, okay? I'm going to miss you. There. I said it. What are you going to do about it?'

'But I'm going to miss you too,' she says simply. 'Of course, I'm going to miss you. But that's not what our marriage should be about, right? I want to live my life and my hopes and my dreams even if it means living away from you for a year or two. And I want you to do the same too, if that's what you want. We'll always have each other to come back to.'

I wish she had written the words down on a greeting card and given it to me so I can go back to it every time I miss her. Instead, she slips her hand under my shirt and draws her index finger down my midriff while looking into my eyes and smiling innocently. I smile too and try to catch her right earlobe between my teeth, but she pushes me back.

'No,' she says and drops her bathrobe to get dressed.

And so it is that half an hour later Ira switches off all the lights in the house one last time, pats Momo as he looks back at her with his baleful mongrel eyes, and steps out on to the landing. As I lock the door, I notice that her gaze lingers on the nameplate we had got made soon after our marriage. We had voted against 'Rohan and Ira' because she had felt that without surnames we sounded like we were of the same breed as Momo. We had voted against 'Shastri and Sebastian' too, because I felt it sounded like I was married to her father. And so it had finally said 'Rohan Shastri and Ira Sebastian', a quirky Kannadiga Hindu and Goan Catholic couple from Bombay in a Jat locality in south Delhi, both secure in their independent identities and the knowledge that they would always have each other to come back to.

*

I get into our second-hand white Alto and immediately turn on the AC. It is past midnight but still quite hot, and lugging Ira's three suitcases that are just under the permissible weight limit has made me sweat. I had insisted on her packing everything from snow boots right down to three packets of Tata Salt so she doesn't have to spend in dollars for a while. I regret all that now as I look at her in the rear-view mirror, waiting for me to reverse the car, and imagine her trying to manage the suitcases by herself all the way from JFK to New Jersey, where she is going to stay with a friend from college for a few weeks before she can find a place of her own, preferably in Manhattan.

Work for the magenta line is going on at Hauz Khas metro station even at this hour. There is some traffic due to the diversions but it's not too bad. The ground rumbles as gigantic machines drill the land. I keep darting glances at Ira as I look at the left side-view mirror. It is difficult to say whether she is nervous, excited or sad, since she's so quiet as she looks out of the window. I place my hand on hers and wait for her to react, but she doesn't.

'You'll manage, right?' I ask, just to break the silence.

'Manage what?'

'Everything. The transfer at London—there isn't much time between the flights. House hunting by yourself in New York. Keeping up with the rest of your class once lectures start. Are you nervous?'

'A little.'

'I worry about you, you know.' I do, but I also know that there is no real reason for me to. She is perfectly capable of finding a nice place to rent, managing her classes and making flight transfers. She likes being independent and by herself.

8

'I know,' she says and gently squeezes my hand without looking at me.

The traffic clears after the IIT flyover. Trucks, allowed within the city at night, drive in the left lane. The road is a little potholed and bumpy, but it's easy to navigate my way around them and hit at least sixty. On any other day I would have loved the drive. But tonight I almost wish there were more traffic so I could stay with Ira a little longer. I let her switch from the old Hindi songs playing on the radio to Frank Sinatra on the pen drive. '*New York, New York*,' he sings, and though the beats are elevating, I feel melancholic.

The road widens after Vasant Vihar and there are only cars headed for the airport. Huge green signboards with white lettering guiding us to T3, the international terminal, loom in the distance. Audis and BMWs whizz past. There is no slowing down now. Soon we take the exit off the Ring Road and enter the airport premises. We pass a line of business hotels, the Delhi Aerocity metro station and bus stops with backlit advertisements. The grounds are so huge that it takes us ten minutes to reach the airport building. The parking charge is Rs 110 for the first half hour and double that for up to two hours. But there is no way I am going to drop Ira off and leave. I go to the basement parking, from where we walk to the departure gate.

We are now surrounded by people saying goodbyes, cheap labour going to the Gulf, families going on foreign holidays. There are the CISF guys manning the gates, looking up from people's IDs and matching their photos with their faces. And there is the brightly lit departure terminal just on the other side of the tall glass walls.

'I'll miss Momo,' Ira says suddenly, and I realize that both of us had been quiet for a long time. It sounds almost like she wants to say she will miss him more than she will miss me. But that can't be what she means and I only smile. 'His shots will be due next month. And don't forget to take him for a walk every morning.'

'I won't,' I say. Any other day I would have told her that I will obviously do these things without being told. But I know this is her way of saying goodbye. Caught up in my own thoughts and trying to see some sign of sadness on her face, I haven't realized that this is harder for her than it is for me.

'Clean the house regularly,' she continues. 'Don't just arrange things in right angles. Clean the exhaust fan in the kitchen before your parents visit. Select a day of the month to pay all the bills so you don't forget. Note down all the expenses in a diary so you know where the money is going.' I don't know what it's like to live in a different country by myself, so I refrain from giving her advice. I know she'll be fine. 'And now get me a trolley.'

I go to the corner where the trolleys are lined up while she waits with her luggage. I turn around and look at her from a distance. This is the last time I will see her for a year. I don't know if by the time she comes back she will have the same wavy, long hair or if she'd have cut and straightened it. If she will lose or gain weight. If she will have an accent. I take in her five-foot-three frame, her narrow waist and firm breasts. She is putting on her sweater in anticipation of the cold inside. She is already preparing for life without me.

I return with the trolley and place her suitcases and handbag on it. We take a selfie in which both of us look more tired and sleep-deprived than sad. My eyes well up again as we hug tight.

'Don't become smug because you are living in New York,' I say without letting go. 'And don't become too comfortable there because you have to come back.'

We kiss, unmindful of the people around.

'I love you,' I say.

I watch her enter through the gate and follow her till I can see her no more. And as I start walking back to the basement parking lot, I am bothered by this feeling that she has left something unsaid.

2
Routine

I wake up the next morning to Momo slobbering all over my face. I push his head away with my hands and try to shove him off the bed with my feet but he does not relent. The room is full of early-morning light. I turn to my left to tell Ira it's Momo's feeding time and realize that her side of the bed is empty. That's when I also realize that I slept through her take-off at four o'clock. I had meant to stay up and wish her a safe journey just before she switched off her phone. I won't say I am paranoid about air travel but it makes me queasy that she will be completely cut off from me for the entire duration of the twenty-hour flight, except for the stopover in London.

I check my phone to see if she has messaged me. She has not. Ira has never set much store by ritualistic things like texting me before take-off. But that's just who she is. I touch her name on the screen in the dialled list and put

12

the phone on speaker. The lady at the other end informs me that the number I am dialling is switched off. I don't know what I had expected.

Perhaps I had just wanted to see her photo appear on the screen. It's a photo I had taken while she was looking away from the camera as we had waited for the food to arrive at this terrace restaurant in Hauz Khas Village called Diagon Alley many months ago. She had just taken a bath before we stepped out and the sun had been mild even though it was afternoon. It had been early winter. She had worn a green kurta and looked fresh—and strikingly pretty—against the trees and the pond that the terrace overlooked.

I miss her already.

Momo is now tugging at my boxers, so I grudgingly climb out of bed. He leads me to his food bowl in the drawing room and nuzzles my hand. I open the cupboard behind me, take out the packet of Pedigree, scoop out some food and deposit it angrily in his bowl. As he starts wolfing down his breakfast, I sit on the floor next to him and stroke his back. I can't be mad at him for long.

I briefly consider going to the balcony in the state I am in. I only need to pick up the newspaper. But Ira has a rule about being decent while opening the door, appearing on the balcony or entertaining guests, no matter how well we know them. So out of deference to her, I put on a T-shirt despite the harsh sun that the balcony faces, and step out. Ira may not be around for a year, but this is our home and her rules still apply.

I settle in the cane lounger and unroll the newspaper. I first look at the headlines, then the strap lines, the graphics, the bullet points and finally the main text of the stories on the front page. There is a misplaced comma here and there but no glaring typos. There will be no fireworks at the evening editorial meeting.

The doorbell rings. That's going to be Shobha, our extremely stern but workaholic Bengali maid who perennially has a wad of paan between her teeth. I open the door, Momo barks, Shobha tells him to shut up without looking at him, and stomps straight off to the kitchen. I open the fridge and look inside for a minute as though I am spoilt for choice and ask her to make bhindi and rotis for lunch and dinner, and butter toast with coffee for breakfast. As I'm about to go to the toilet, 'Where is didi?' Shobha demands.

If it were any other maid, I would have found the question intrusive and told her off. But I am used to Shobha's ways by now and don't mind them because she is a good cook, punctual, rarely goes on leave and positively *asks* to be given clothes to wash. Also, she is the only one with the temperament to go about the house cooking and cleaning without being unnerved by Momo, who likes to stalk and stare.

'She's gone,' I say simply. 'She told you yesterday. She has gone to America to study.'

Shobha looks at me very judgementally without saying anything. Ira had in fact informed her, but perhaps Shobha finds it impossible to believe that a woman would leave her husband behind unchecked and go to another

country. In any case, without elaborating on the status of our marriage, I go to the toilet and sit on the pot to prepare myself for the day.

*

I am flooded with calls and messages the entire morning. Amma calls me to ask if Ira has landed in London. But I know that she knows that the flight does not land for another hour. She has actually called to check if I sound sad. Mummy calls too, asks me baldly if I am missing Ira and laughs. Daddy calls and hangs up in eleven seconds. He usually speaks to his daughter for sixteen, so I am not offended. Appa calls an hour later to inform me that the flight has landed. I know that he knows that I am tracking the flight online. But I appreciate that he wants me to know that he is too.

It's noon. It has been forty-five minutes since Google showed me that Ira's flight landed in London, and I am waiting for her call. I try calling her several times but can't get through. There's no message from her either. WhatsApp says that her Last Seen was at 3.56 a.m. I am going to start panicking soon and switch on a news channel. Then I think of checking my email and see that there is indeed one from Ira.

'Don't panic,' it reads. 'Can't get network on the phone. Writing from a kiosk at the airport. Landed half an hour back. Flight was comfortable, slept throughout. First world is nice.' That is it. I smile at the 'Don't panic', then feel miffed by the telegrammatic tone of the email. But mostly I am glad that the plane hasn't crashed.

Two hours later, while I am having lunch and falling head over heels in love with Amy Poehler as I watch *Parks and Recreation* on my laptop, Yusuf messages me on WhatsApp.

'Has the wife left?'

'Yea. All alone now.' I keep it short, not wanting to sound overly dramatic.

Yusuf was just an acquaintance from journalism school before he agreed to take me in as his roommate on Ira's request when I first moved to Delhi. He and Ira were good friends, and continue to be—only that he and I too are close now; he was my 'best man' at our court wedding. Last year he moved to a high-paying job with Reuters in Bangalore, where he stays with his girlfriend Mira. At thirty he does not look a day older than seventeen, is the kindest, wisest person I know and is full of cheer at all hours of the day. Which is how I can get away with saying things like 'All alone now' to him without him getting unduly worried for me.

'Oh dear,' he replies. 'What will you do for sex now?'

I smile. It's just the sort of thing he would say to lighten the mood.

'Good question. And thanks for asking. Everyone is making this all about Ira. Where she will live, how she will get by, New York is so expensive, etcetera. No one stops to ask what I will do when I get horny.' Then I add, 'On second thoughts, maybe that's a good thing.'

'Ha! So what *will* you do when you get horny? And remember, I owe allegiance to you and Ira both, so

16

whatever you say to me will be passed on to her. Though I'd say the time is ripe for a sordid office affair. Didn't you tell me about a cute girl?'

'Alisha? Yards out of my league.'

'Hmm. I'm sure I can hook you up with someone real nice.'

'Do. Do. But I don't know how you'll sell me. I doubt if they'll even do it for money.'

'Hey! You're a catch. I'll be sending.'

'I'll be waiting,' I reply.

The conversation ends there, and I realize that I'm taking myself less seriously now than I did yesterday, thanks to the faux locker-room talk. I know Yusuf looks out for me and Ira, and worries about what the distance will do to our marriage as much as our parents do, but he prefers to keep the tone light. And I'm grateful to him for that.

By the time I leave for work at four, Ira's flight has taken off from London. On the first floor I ring Sunil's doorbell; he is particular about getting his rent on the thirtieth of the month. His son Varun opens the door.

'Rent,' I announce. He goes in and sends his mother to the door. She takes the money from me and counts the notes carefully.

Just when I am about to leave, she asks, 'Why was Ira crying last night?'

'It wasn't her, it was me.'

Anju looks amused. 'Your wife makes you cry?' She sounds as though she and Ira could form a group, and I feel my heart go out to Sunil.

17

'She left for America last night. She is going to study there for two years.'

Her face also expresses the same disapproval that Shobha's did. 'Your dog barks too much,' she says. I mumble something about running late for office and rush downstairs.

*

At work, there is such an overwhelming amount of concern being expressed to my face and whispered behind my back that I start to feel obligated to be in mourning. It's not just my colleagues on the front-page desk who know about Ira's move to New York. Everyone in city, nation and world knows too. And everyone in design. And they all make it a point to ask me how I am doing. I get the impression that perhaps some of them believe Ira and I have separated and are simply refusing to admit it to the world. Those who seem to think our marriage is still on, especially the women, make sombre faces and hold my hand in solidarity.

'Let me tell you in all honesty, Rohan,' says a reporter, 'how lucky I think your wife is. I wish my husband had let me study in the US. I could have been working for the *New York Times* today.' I want to tell her Ira is not lucky but talented. If anything, she should praise her for the full tuition fee waiver she got.

A senior male editor says, 'You are a good man, Rohan, for allowing your wife to go away and do what she wants.' I want to tell him how patriarchal that sounds but think better of it.

An old hand in design says, 'Why didn't you go to New York? What great career are you building here?'

'Who will give me a job there, dada?' I reply, because he likes it when people sound weary and defeated like him. 'And without that, how will we pay off the loan?'

The only one to act as though nothing remarkable has happened is Tanuj. He works at the terminal next to mine and is the only one in editorial my age. By default that means I'm closest to him in office. He looks up as I sit down in my chair and says, 'Hey.' He acknowledges what is going on in my mind with the offer of a sympathetic fist bump and leaves it at that.

'There's been a triple murder in Gurgaon,' he informs me. 'Man kills wife, son and self because of financial problems. Front-page flier.' And with that I get down to business.

In the deadline-driven rush at the national headquarters of *The Fourth Estate*, I lose track of time. It helps. But I also almost ignore the message on WhatsApp at midnight from an unknown number. Then I remember Ira and look closely. 'Landed an hour back. Message me when you're done with work. This is my new number.'

We just have minutes before the front-page needs to be in press. But I first assign the Diagon Alley photo to the new number so I don't ever ignore it again. And only then do I get back to work.

3
Change

Ira slips into her new and exciting life as easily as though she had been preparing for it the whole time. I had expected her to take at least a week to overcome the jet lag and orient herself to a new culture before moving out of her friend's place in New Jersey and begin looking for a flat. But within the first four days, she has shifted to a house on Christie Street in the Lower East Side.

An artist she knew from the time she worked at an art gallery in Delhi recommended her to a seventy-year-old artist friend, Laura, who lives alone in a two-bedroom apartment. She offered Ira her spare room for six hundred dollars. It does not take me much time to calculate that that translates into almost a full month's salary for me. But Ira assures me that she could not have found a place so close to her school for anything less than two thousand dollars.

Ira sends me photos of the house and also takes me on a virtual tour of it on a video call. The place looks extremely cluttered to me but Ira tells me the clutter is part of the character of the apartment.

'There are things here that lost their function forty years ago,' she says, not disapprovingly. 'Laura's husband, Hanz, who was also an artist, died of lung cancer some years ago. They suspect it had something to do with the toxic air following the WTC crashes on 9/11. Laura says his two-year battle was difficult but he was cheerful throughout—because he had survived the Second World War in Germany and after that found no experience in life unbearable. He escaped to New York a few months before the war ended. The things you see around the house are things he collected then onwards. He never threw them away because, Laura says, they reminded him of a place that is safe.'

Laura also has a tabby cat called Estelle. Ira tells me that she too has had a difficult childhood. She grew up in an animal shelter where she had to compete with twenty full-grown cats for food. Which meant she had to gobble it fast. And though she now lives in a house where three meals a day are guaranteed, she continues to eat so quickly that she often throws up and needs to be fed in tiny quantities. The first few days, she was scared of Ira and kept her distance, but has since warmed up to her. The only problem with that is that Ira's room is not actually a room. It has been created by partitioning off a part of the house with paper walls. Estelle likes to visit by walking straight through the walls and does not believe in using the same opening twice. Other than that, she is well behaved and does not create a needless ruckus like our stud back home.

A few days later Ira shows me how she has done up her room. It does look more homely now. She has decorated it with photos and artworks that she found lying around the house. They are stunning pieces of work, especially this one photograph of a young boy sitting in his father's lap and looking straight at the camera. His mother is seated on a couch in the background and is looking at the camera too. You can sense they are poor but there is something defiant about them.

'Rohan,' Ira says into the phone that night—her night, my day. 'We will not raise our children like other people do. They will sit in my lap whenever they feel like and have adult food. They will grow up with cats and dogs and any other animal they want. They can choose to not study maths or English if they don't feel like it. They will walk naked if they want to and will not tie their hair if they don't want to.' So the decency rules apply only to me, is it, I want to ask her, but I don't because I like the sound of her voice and the things she is saying. 'There will be no bare walls in our house. They will be filled with curiosities from around the world. Each morning, my children and I should be able to lose ourselves studying a different part of the wall. There need to be enough parts to keep us occupied for years.'

I don't reply. I had no idea she had such specific thoughts on the topic. 'Even when I was nine I was thinking about how I will raise my children,' she says.

'I don't know whether I ever want to have children. But I definitely don't want to have them and raise them in a house whose walls are filled with shadows.'

I had asked her the question several times before but never got a proper answer: what did her interest in art stem from? I wonder now if this is what led her to study art, if it's the same thing that made an artist out of Hanz. Only such a person would want to create something who has seen so much around him destroyed. Only she would look for beauty who has shadows to fill.

*

It's hard for me to keep track of Ira's classmates. They become a jumble of names and nationalities. I know there is a Gloria, a Liz, a Stuart, a Marion, a Malcolm and a Xavier. I know there is a Brazilian, a Lebanese, an Ecuadorian, an American and a French. But if I were to match the two columns, I'd fail, considering I just recounted one nationality less than the names.

I use pegs to remember her professors. There is the dean who gave her the full tuition fee waiver and whose expectations she is now desperately trying to live up to. Then there is a professor from Australia who, she thinks, looks a lot like me. A third, a woman, is extremely fond of Ira and always has positive things to say about every assignment she turns in. I do not doubt Ira's talent, but I like to tease her by suggesting that her professor's appreciation stems from the correctness of being nice to a third-world citizen.

For me it's strange to not be able to construct her new life in my head. When she was in Delhi, I knew her colleagues well. I had met them several times and was familiar with their voices and habits. I knew Ira's routine after she left from office in the evening. I knew she would walk from Lajpat Nagar out to the Ring Road and look for an auto. After reaching Shahpur Jat, she would buy vegetables from the vendor right under our balcony, groceries from the store in the back lane and milk from the Mother Dairy outlet across the road. I knew she would come home, have a shower, heat the morning's food in the microwave, feed Momo and then have dinner while watching *Bob's Burgers* on her laptop. Then she would go to sleep and stir briefly when I reached home at midnight. But I'm at a loss now. I know she takes the subway to and back from school, that she picks up something cheap to eat at the Lebanese cart near her place and does her assignments after reaching her room. But never having seen any of it myself, I'm not able to recreate her world.

New York grows on Ira rather quickly. She tells me that everything costs a million dollars and there are an insane number of homeless people in the city, all of whom are necessarily black. 'But even though it's a crowded city, people actually greet each other,' she says. 'I mean strangers greet each other. Today alone I had one cop, one garbage collector, one passenger in the train and two kids greet me. And you know those super annoying people in their cars on the streets of Delhi who don't let you cross in peace even on a zebra crossing during a red light? They should all be sent here. Cars here go at ten miles per hour and they wait for every single human being to cross before starting the engine.'

She feels safe in New York in a way she never did in Delhi or even in Bombay. The subway runs all night and I don't worry when she returns from pubs after a night out with her friends at one or two. What she likes most about the city is that everyone walks a lot. And they eat and drink as they walk. It's a city full of really busy people from all over the world and they let you be.

'They let you *be*,' she emphasizes. 'It's a city that does not judge you, a place where all the deviants in the world can assemble without making heads turn. You can be a cultural, a racial or a sexual minority and no one will look at you weirdly. You can be a single woman or a single parent and the landlord won't threaten to call up your parents if you are a thirty-year-old guy getting a girl home.' Then she says something that leaves me feeling melancholic but I'm sure she didn't mean it that way: 'It's where one can come just to be left alone.'

For me, it's difficult to break out of the habit of having her around and be left alone, but it's not like I regret not being in New York. I like the life I have built for myself in Delhi. I like my routine of waking up at eight to Momo, going to office in the afternoon and returning home at night with the satisfaction of having sent an edition to press. I like driving my Alto on roads I have grown familiar with. A few years ago I may have but now I don't feel sorry for myself that *I* didn't get a chance to study in Manhattan, that I can't even hope to get a job in New York. I do not feel like I'm missing out on the vastness of Central Park or the redness of maple trees in autumn. More than not being drawn to New York, I think the thing that keeps me in Delhi is that I'm really attached to this place. For me, Delhi is my city of love.

4
Delhi

Yes, come to think of it, that's how I'll put it. I don't know if it's true for others also, if they too have a certain place they associate completely with the security and happiness of love. But, for me, there is such a place, and that is Delhi. To be correct, Delhi was not where Ira and I first met or where we first started dating. That was Bombay. But then we broke up and got back together only after she had moved here to study at JNU, both of us realizing too late that we were more attached to each other than we knew.

Just at the onset of winter that year, I told Amma and Appa that there was an office conference I had to attend in Delhi, and flew down to spend a few days with Ira. It was a beautiful time—thin wisps of fog curling around trees in the wide, quiet roads of the city under a sun that was tender even at noon. Ira hadn't yet got her hostel room at the time. She shared a third-floor barsati in

Munirka with a classmate who, Ira told me, had cleared out for the weekend after telling her to 'make good use of it'. But by the time we got to her place after lunch, I was so tired from having woken up early for the flight that I fell asleep on the mattress on the floor without meaning to. I woke up at some point to the sound of her making tea. She didn't realize I was up, so I watched her. The sun was setting in the window in front of her. She shimmered. And when she turned around, she was surprised to find me looking at her.

In the evening, she took me to JNU for a walk. She was so happy there that I was fond of it already. I rubbed my hands as we entered through the gate and dug them deep into the pockets of my sweatshirt. We walked down the main road of the campus as she pointed out the hostels named after rivers; the health centre where treatment was practically free; Ganga dhaba, where she had lemon tea in paper cups morning and night; the shopping centre, where a Tibetan joint had cheap but good food and where I had momos for the first time in my life.

The next day Ira wanted to show me Delhi. The reason I had come prepared to like the city was that she liked it already. But I also fell in love with its tree-lined roads and the metro, which, to me, stood for something other than itself. The crowded lanes of Chandni Chowk felt like home. At Jama Masjid we took selfies, though the word wasn't coined yet, with my clunky point-and-shoot camera. We didn't pose or make faces at the camera, only brought our heads together in an arch and smiled. When I look back at the photos today, we look happy. Whether we knew it or not back then I don't know, but we weren't simply dating. We were in love.

For dinner she took me to Hauz Khas Village. There were barely three restaurants there at the time and we went to the rooftop of one. Ira told me there was a huge park with a small pond just behind the village. Of course, in the dark I could make out neither, but knowing they were there made me feel like I had come somewhere far from the city. We ate quickly and left as the place became deserted at nine. Also, since it was my last night in Delhi, I was cold with eagerness to get back.

But it's not simply because I went through a rite of passage in Delhi that I call it my city of love. It's because when I think of Delhi, I think of two- and three-storied structures built very close to each other, of rooftops overlooking unseen parks and ponds, of noisy lanes leading up to the tranquillity of a masjid, of roads smelling of new-born amaltas at the start of winter and of bodies colliding in a fever in the dead of quiet night. And all of it is tinged with the mellow, yellow tones of love.

*

I moved to Delhi the next year. It was a jerky start to a new phase in life. The houses around the North Campus of DU, where I had enrolled for a master's, were tiny and expensive. For a month, I moved around from the house of one acquaintance to another, until their patience ran out. But I had no luck finding a good place. Then one day Ira told me a room in a two-bedroom house in upmarket Vasant Enclave where Yusuf was staying had fallen vacant and I could move in with him. The only problem was it would be twenty-odd kilometres from North Campus. But I decided to take it anyway. I was tired of the house hunt and the place was close to JNU, where Ira now had a hostel room.

The master's itself was a let-down. Having had a job for two years, I sorely missed the clink of salary in my bank account every month. And I discovered my heart was no longer in academics, least of all in a class with a hundred others. But the worst of it was that Ira was so occupied with her submissions for her final semester that she could not make much time for me. The only thing that kept me going in those difficult first few months was the ever-friendly presence of Yusuf. He had been little more than a flatmate at the time but would drop by my room every night after returning from work just to ask how my day had been, and in that daily small act of kindness I found comfort.

'I've decided to move back to Bombay,' I went to him and announced dramatically one night after I was sure we had become friends, my eyes a fierce shade of red.

Even though he was on a video call with Mira, he saw I was visibly upset and called me in. And I poured out all that had gone wrong in the last few months. 'On the basis of all you've just told me,' he said seriously with the air of a psychologist making his diagnosis, 'I think you are very much in need of a dog. Have you ever had one or considered getting one?'

'What?'

'You have just moved to a new city, you are returning to academics, your whole life has changed. Of course, you'll need some time to get used to it. But that's it. If you move back to Bombay, you'll only end up feeling like a loser for having dropped out. Let Ira be. She needs to focus on her studies. Create a new life for yourself here. Give yourself some time to settle in. And do get a dog, really! If you're lonely and going through a phase, having one around always helps. Like, *always*! In the meantime, I'm going to send you YouTube links to the tracks of an Icelandic band called Sigur Ros. Listen to them.'

That night I went to bed listening to '*Hoppipolla*' on loop, only the happiest piece of music I've heard to date. And over the next few weeks things started to look up. Our house was on the ground floor, and as if she had overheard Yusuf's suggestion to me, one day a dog walked into our veranda with two newborn pups. I started looking after them in her absence, and caring for them was somehow therapeutic for me. I also decided to get a full-time job to keep me occupied while I did the master's. When Yusuf moved to Bangalore to be with Mira, he recommended me for the position he was leaving at the *Estate*.

Soon I was attending classes in the morning, going for work in the afternoon and returning home late at night. My days were just packed. It gave me this heady feeling I loved despite the exhaustion. By the time I completed the master's, I felt I had done so much with life that the only thing left was marriage. I had known Ira for twelve years and the time felt right. One night on an impulse I showed up outside her hostel and went down on a knee. My desk job did not let me afford jewellery, so I slipped the ring of a keychain on her finger.

'I haven't got much by way of money or talent,' I said. 'But I promise you a life of unwavering commitment and freedom to pursue whatever you please. I will fill your life with happiness or die trying. You have given me such joy and stability that I cannot imagine being with anybody else. Ira Sebastian, will you marry me?' She, of course, found the whole thing rather ridiculous and did not hesitate to say so. She hemmed and hawed, but in the end, she did not say no.

*

I nervously went to Bombay for a few days with the secret intention of announcing our decision to Amma and Appa. I wasn't sure how they were going to react. But every time I've underestimated my parents, I've regretted it. And so it was this time too. We went out for lunch one day, and Amma must have read the anxiety on my face.

'What have you decided to do after your master's?' she asked and gave me the opening I was looking for.

'To get married,' I said, and there was something in their expressions that told me they were prepared for this. Perhaps they knew about Ira too.

Appa grabbed my hand and, laughing heartily, said, 'Congratulations!'

And that was it. No questions about whether we had thought this through. No objections, not even tentative ones. For our engagement, we called just those who would be earnestly happy for us. Other than family, we only really cared about having Yusuf there. We debated whether the ceremony three months later should be Hindu, Catholic or both but finally agreed on a court wedding. And so with signatures in a register in the middle of a humid working day in Bombay in June, and after exchanging garlands on a podium in a government office with our parents as witnesses and Yusuf as best man, we were married.

When we returned to Delhi, we went straight to the Shahpur Jat house which Ira and I had selected just before leaving for Bombay for the wedding. Gaurav, a close friend of Ira's from JNU, had moved our things while we were away. He had also ensured that we arrived to a bed covered with rose petals. Ira and I spent that month setting up our first home, growing closer as we picked curtains, bought a bed and merged our collections of books into one shelf. That month I woke up and went to bed day after day with the firm conviction that this joy would last forever. When I look back I feel it was the time of my life. And it was all in Delhi, my city of love.

5
Fight

I am Facebook's perfect husband because it's not enough for me to miss my wife. I must also tell the world. I take down my profile photo in which I look like Rajesh Khanna in *Aradhana*. It was taken on a trek to Triund in the Himachal mountains five years ago and had been up since then because I am so fond of it. It is a huge step for me to replace it now with the one in which I look tired and sleep-deprived: the selfie Ira and I took at the airport. This photo gets me more than a hundred likes, a big number for a Facebook-unpopular person like me. And what helps me get them are the comments.

A cousin identifies it as an airport farewell shot even though there isn't much of the background visible. 'Hope Ira has reached safely. So proud of you guys. Xoxo,' she writes.

To which a long-lost friend from school replies, 'Hey, how you been? It's been ages. Where's your wife? And congratulations on the wedding, by the way!'

'In NYC. Studying,' I reply.

That lets the word out to everyone well outside the family and my small circle of friends. Granduncles, ex-college professors and people I did not know I had on my friends' list ask me what Ira has gone to study, how long she will be there and why I haven't tagged along. It's basically a replay of what happened on my first day in office after Ira left, just on a much wider and more public scale. And the attention doesn't bother me any more. On the other hand, it encourages me to step things up.

I start a series of daily posts on Facebook with the hashtag #Wordsthatmademethinkofyoutoday. The idea occurs to me one day when I'm driving to work and 'Tire Swing', the song from *Juno*, comes on the radio. The first two lines of the second stanza sound like they were written for Ira and me:

> '*Cause I like to be gone most of the time*
> *And you like to be home most of the time.*'

I imagine Ira waking up to see herself tagged in the post with multiple likes. I imagine my public displays of affection making her feel happy and loved. I am about to go to sleep that night after returning from work when my phone buzzes and I see that she has liked the post. 'I like to be home too,' she replies, and my friends go wild liking her comment now.

Next, from Jhumpa Lahiri's *The Namesake*, one of my all-time favourite novels, I quote: 'You are still young, free. Do yourself a favour. Before it's too late, without thinking too much about it first, pack a pillow and a blanket and see as much of the world as you can. You will not regret it. One day it will be too late.'

I dig out her post on my wall from more than a year ago, which she had written to make me feel better after some trouble in office, and quote it back to her, with the same hashtag, of course: 'I love how you curl up next to Momo and I love on most days how you look at me when I'm talking but you don't hear a word. I love that you make your own breakfast and let me sleep. And I love the poems you write for me. We are un-jinxable because we have each other.'

I did not have a smartphone before Ira left for New York. But when she left she gave me hers, saying she would have to buy a new one there anyway. One day I go through the WhatsApp groups that she was part of and whose messages she has not deleted. There is a group of her friends from college in which she had written on the day she left, 'I'm leaving Rohan in your care. Do make sure I don't have to read headlines like, "Lonely man found under heaps of doggy poop."' The thought of her looking out for me in her absence is overwhelming. I take a screenshot of the message and save it on the phone but don't post it. This one I keep for myself.

*

'Can't sleep, I'm very awake.'

I wake up to this WhatsApp message at 4.30 one morning, read it drowsily and then doze back off. It's six-thirty when I wake up next and see that the message is from Yusuf. Since he alternately does morning, afternoon and night shifts at the Reuters newsroom in Bangalore, he sometimes has trouble falling asleep during the transitions, and I'm used to receiving texts from him at odd hours. The message is followed by YouTube links to three songs.

'I'm up now,' I reply, 'though I don't know if you are. Are you?'

'I am! I am!' he replies, almost instantly.

'Oh boy, tonight must be difficult. So what are these songs?'

'It's three parts of a long symphony by this British rock band called Muse. The band's lead vocalist, Matthew Bellamy, says it's a story of humanity coming to an end and everyone resting their hopes on some astronauts who go out to space to spread humanity on another planet.'

'Interesting.'

'It is! It made me think of you—of us. I wanted to tell you about this thought I had while listening to the tracks.'

'Go on.'

'I think if we are ever in a war, like the First World War or the Second Peloponnesian War, you and I will be the last people of a platoon left. Because, let's face it, we're awesome. So, we are the last people left fighting and then you'll tell me that I need to run and save myself and I'll

37

be like no. But you'll be like go and have lots of sex and read a lot of graphic novels. You'll tell me to name my kid after you. And I'll ask, which one. You'll say, every third one. And I'll have to listen to you and leave you on the battlefield alone. The enemy will advance since you're fighting alone and all but then you'll see that I've come back. We shall fight together.'

It makes me smile and I tell him it reminds me of *The Lord of the Rings*. 'How Sam comes back to save Frodo. Frodo may be the star of the story, but I think of Sam as the greater hero for not letting the ring overpower him and because he is a true friend. So thanks for coming back for me.'

'We live such exciting lives, Rohan,' he says with a touch of irony. 'There will be a movie made about us some day. Who would you want to play you onscreen?'

'Who, me? Never thought about it. Maybe Rajesh Khanna the romantic from *Aradhana*.'

*

Soon it's November, the month I like best in Delhi. The long transition through October from the muggy monsoon months is over. Last night, a dreamy mist stole up on me as I was walking through the park outside Hauz Khas metro station, which means winter has arrived. I think the furtive sun of November makes us a happy lot. Shopkeepers and auto drivers are more pleasant to customers. There are more people out on the India Gate lawns. And it's not like they are ever out of season, but now is when you enjoy momos the most.

Delhi rubs off on me too. The sadness of Ira leaving is behind me, and I'm feeling well settled in my new routine. Snug in some new woollens, I go on long walks with Momo, sometimes as far as Deer Park. He likes the weather too. He makes fewer attempts to break free and run off, instead walking in step with me. I've got us identical red coats, an 'I' for Ira knitted on the back of his and on the chest of mine. We look like buddies out for a good time around town. And a good time we have, admiring the pretty ones of our respective species.

My productivity also shoots up. Just before Diwali, I spend a lot of time cleaning the house. And to mark the occasion, I repost on Facebook last year's photo of Ira, her face aglow, lighting a diya in our dark balcony, with the caption, 'This Diwali, we'll get by on happy memories from last Diwali.'

On days the car cleaner doesn't turn up, I clean my Alto myself and do a thorough job of it, washing the floor mats and the wheel caps too. One day I overhear Anju telling Sunil in the balcony to learn from me and get some exercise, instead of adding an inch to his considerable waist every month.

'Just see how well he can manage without his wife. And you,' she admonishes, 'you can't even pick out your own underwear without yelling Anju, Anju. Nor do you have any appreciation for the wife who does that for you.' He listens to the tirade peaceably and bravely but shoots me an angry look on my way up.

And I socialize, something I haven't done in years. The last time must have been when Ira was in JNU and I would invite her friends over for poker nights on weekends, hoping to fit better in her world. Since then I have forgotten what it is like to hang out with people other than Ira.

One afternoon, Tanuj and I decide to go to Old Delhi before heading to work. Like me, he is also from Bombay and a single man living by himself in the city. We discover that we have more things in common than we knew. We both like exploring the city and looking for cheap places to eat good food, and realize that we can be tolerable travel companions with an equal appreciation of a well-prepared shahi tukda.

On my day off the following week, I decide to catch up with Gaurav in JNU, where he is now reluctantly doing an MPhil to avoid getting a job.

'Hey, roomie!' he says brightly as he opens the door of his hostel room and hugs me. We were roommates once for a short while after Yusuf had moved out and I was yet to get married.

'Were you smoking up?' I say as I see his glassy eyes. He grunts and returns to the game he is playing on his laptop. I boss him around and give him life advice as though he were the younger brother I always wished I had, while he wishes me away like he would his father—an old equation neither of us has been able to outgrow.

'Come, let's go to 24x7. I'm in the mood for some butter chicken,' I say.

'Your treat? I'm broke.'

'Yes, all right.'

Over cups of lemon tea and plates of spicy chicken in the biting cold, he tells me about one girl he is sleeping with, a second he wants to get back with, and a third he wants to hook up with—all in one breath—as I silently tune in and out, feeling indulgent and jealous in turn. We then go back to his room and open a bottle of Old Monk, of which he is never in short supply no matter how broke, and I return home well after two.

*

One night the next week, I'm leaving from office when I see Alisha seeming a little lost and worried as she stands at the gate looking at the deserted road outside. This is unlike her usual self. Lean, tall and always in jeans and T-shirts, she otherwise comes across as a hardy woman of the world. From whatever I've heard from others in the team, she is from Jaipur but grew up in towns and cities around the world, travelling with her diplomat mother, and has lived all her adult life by herself, going on Himalayan treks alone every couple of weeks. I've never really spoken to her, even though she works on the state desk in my adjoining bay.

'Hey,' I say to her on my way to the parking lot across the road. Since the desk works well into the night, we get a cab drop home, though I prefer taking my Alto. 'Everything all right? You seem hassled.'

'Hey,' she replies absent-mindedly, without looking at me, 'missed my office drop. And there aren't any Olas or Ubers at this hour.'

'I can drop you if you like. Mayur Vihar is out of the way, but won't take long without traffic.'

'I don't live in Mayur Vihar,' she suddenly rounds on me and says.

'Oh,' I blush, 'I just thought I had heard you mention at some point—some time when they were announcing office cabs perhaps.'

'Used to—when I stayed with my boyfriend. But then I broke up with him,' she says with a disarming smile and I feel embarrassed. 'It reminds me too much of my life with him. So I moved south some time back. Anyway, there are more things to do there and I find it safer.'

'That's true. Where in south?'

'Green Park.'

'Oh, that's only a short detour on my way home then. I can drop you.'

She looks a little hesitant. 'That'll be great,' she says eventually and starts walking ahead of me towards the parking lot. 'These guys take a long route, you know. Dropping off all the seniors first. Takes me twice the time it should.'

'That's horrible.'

'How's your wife? I hear she is studying in New York. Ira, right?' she asks as she gets into the car, almost as if to make sure I'm committed to her despite the distance so she doesn't need to feel threatened.

'She's good. Settling into a routine and getting really busy with her assignments.'

'That's nice. You should tell her to try out this chain of French restaurants in Manhattan, Maison Kayser.

They're really good. I used to eat there almost every day when I lived in New York as a teen. You guys Skype every day?' Again I get the same impression.

'Not really. She has unlimited international calling on her phone. I message her and she calls. But she's mostly busy through the week. Then there's the time difference.'

'That must suck.'

'Sort of. But we're in a good place,' I say, and I'm taken aback by my choice of words. I wonder if I really said it to reassure myself more than her.

Thanks to the traffic-free roads at night, we reach Green Park in less than fifteen minutes. After she has stepped out, I feel amused by the way our clumsy conversation had lapsed into an awkward silence, both of us pretending to listen to the songs playing on the radio. I reason that she must still be smarting from her break-up and I can see why she would want to keep her distance from all men for a while.

But the next day we bump into each other in the office cafeteria; we are both there to grab a cup of tea and a sandwich just before office hours. And soon it turns into a routine—Alisha and I catching up for a few minutes over tea in the cafe before heading to our floor.

*

Saying it out loud to Alisha sets me thinking. I hadn't paid much attention to it but I do now: how Ira and I don't talk every day. How, when we do, it's always me who messages her and asks her to call. And how short these calls always are. Earlier I had put it down to

43

her being busy with her assignments, as I said to Alisha. But increasingly I find myself thinking about Ira—while sitting at my terminal and editing a story, while having tea with Alisha, while stroking Momo as he eats—and debating if this is something I should talk to Ira about.

It is December now, and there is a deathly quiet all around. It's like everyone in the city is putting their energy into staying warm and nothing else. My house too feels eerily silent. Shobha is wrapped up in a sweater and a shawl, her body bent against the cold wind, as she appears at my door every morning and goes about her work wordlessly. Momo sleeps through most of the day, occasionally barking at night in response to the stray dogs outside. Varun no longer appears shirtless on the balcony after returning home from school to allow himself to be seen by the gaggle of girls in uniform passing by. The season for doing so had long gone but he had persisted, perhaps in the hope of getting lucky and boasting to his friends, who come on expensive bikes in the dead of night. Now, he too has retreated to the warmth of clothes and a house whose doors stay shut.

I am startled out of sleep one night by someone at the door ringing the bell not once, not twice but six or seven times in succession. I jump and sit up in bed wide awake. I switch on the light and see it's four-fifteen. Whoever is at the door is really angry. Or dying. Or maybe the building is on fire. Momo is already at the door, barking loudly. I am a little wary of opening it because there's no safety door outside. There's no option but to open it.

44

It's Anju. Wrapped up from head to toe, in the dark she looks like an apparition. And she looks scary because she is livid. 'That dog,' she snarls, and I push Momo away from the door. 'It has been barking for one hour along with its friends on the road. How do you expect your neighbours to sleep through this noise?'

'Sorry,' I say, hoping it will placate her. I am shivering, not just because I have forgotten to wear my sweatshirt in the rush to open the door but also because I do not respond well to people yelling at me, certainly not at four-fifteen in the morning. 'It's just that it's winter and you hear the barking since the fans and ACs are off.'

'Of course, I know that. But just because your dog has been barking all year does not make it okay for him to keep us up tonight. Make it stop or I will have it thrown out.' With that, she turns around and stomps off.

Just then Momo barks at her and I quickly close the door, making sure I lock it properly. I retrieve his toy bone from under the bed and throw it at him. He catches it in his mouth and his barking stops as he starts chewing it. I go back to bed but my shivering doesn't stop despite the blanket. I am unable to sleep, so I decide to call Ira.

'Hello? Why are you up so early?' she asks.

'Just had a huge fight with Anju. Momo was barking and she came to complain. Rang the bell ten times and threatened to have him thrown out.'

'It's all right. She'll be fine tomorrow. She's not going to throw him out. Talk to her calmly in the morning.'

She is talking in a soft whisper, which annoys me. 'Where are you?' I demand.

'In the library. Listen, I have an assignment to submit in an hour. Go back to sleep and we'll talk later.'

And before I can check myself, I scream louder than Anju. 'Talk to me now! I am sick of you telling me you can't talk because of some stupid assignment.'

Ira does not respond immediately. I hear her shuffling around and figure she must be stepping out of the library. 'Don't talk to me like that, Rohan,' she says loud and clear. 'You know Momo starts barking when he doesn't have his toys around. Why didn't you make sure before going to sleep that he had his bone with him?'

'I did. He had it,' I lie because I don't want to admit that she knows well what's happening in our house despite being on a different continent.

'Whatever that is, this is part of having a pet. There will be days when you have to face the neighbours.'

'That's rich, considering you are the one who got Momo home in the first place.' I regret saying it as soon as the words leave my mouth; I remember well why she had decided to get Momo home.

I flare up quickly and calm down quickly too. But I know that Ira, once angry, can remain angry for days. 'Listen, I don't want to fight,' I say in a conciliatory tone. 'I can manage the Momo situation. I just got upset and expected you to talk to me properly for five minutes without using your assignments as an excuse and trying to hang up.'

'Don't talk dismissively about my work. It's important to me. It's what I've come here to do.'

'I'm not dismissive of your work.'

'You are. You always have been. You did this to me in JNU also. I got top grades in my first year when you were not in Delhi. And as soon as you arrived, they started slipping. You just don't think what I do is important. You always want me to keep it aside and focus on you. Your argument with Anju. Your work. You should listen to yourself when you're in office and I call you. You cut the call without even checking whether what I have called to say is urgent.'

'That's different. I can't stop press because you want to talk to me. I have a deadline,' I say and know immediately what she is going to say.

'And I don't? I also have to submit my assignment in an hour. The entire class is sitting in the library. Half of them are having meltdowns. You live in your cosy dream world where you think posting romantic things on Facebook every day makes you a good husband. Let me break it to you, Rohan. It doesn't. You do it only to make yourself look good in front of the world. But it doesn't do anything for me.'

I can feel my temper rising. 'Why are you making this about other things? I was just a bit upset and wanted to talk to you for five minutes so I could calm down and go back to sleep, which I wasn't able to.'

'Instead you yelled at me and upset me and made sure I won't be able to concentrate and turn in my assignment on time. This is what you do. This is what you've done all the time. Why call me with a problem when you don't want my help? I told you to talk to Anju tomorrow after both of you have calmed down. What more can I do when I'm in a different country?'

'And whose fault is that?'

'What do you mean?'

'Nothing.'

'No, tell me. Tell me what you mean. Don't be shy.'

'Don't be nasty, Ira. I didn't mean anything.'

'No, you did. You always do.'

'Fine. You're the one who has made the choice to leave your husband behind and fly off to live your dream. The least you can do is make five minutes for me when I need you. Let me figure in your scheme of things.'

'For twelve years you've figured in my scheme of things. Not just figured, you *were* my scheme of things. I used to hang around you the entire time in college. Write the assignments you would submit in your name. But were you there for me when I needed you?'

I don't respond because I don't know what she is talking about. She continues.

'Or were you too selfish to notice all the times I cried myself to sleep for a year after we got married? No, you weren't even home all those times. You were in office sending your paper to press.'

'What are you talking about?'

'For a year I tried to tell you how depressed I was in my job. I kept telling you I wanted to quit. And all you ever asked me was how we were going to pay the rent. And that too was something you said on the days you bothered to respond. The rest of the time you only behaved like everyone has problems at work and I should chin up and pull my weight in the house. So don't ask me whose fault it is that I'm in a different country. Because it isn't mine.'

'What's that supposed to mean?' I ask her quietly.

And the few moments she takes to reply tell me that it is a conscious decision she has made to say what she says; she is not saying it out of anger.

'You know, there are times when my friends make sad faces at me and tell me it must be so difficult for me to stay away from you. And I play along and say yes. But I feel rotten inside because it's not true. I love you but I miss Momo more. When I think about our marriage, I only feel bad that it's reduced to this. Of course, I wanted to study in New York, but I came here because I couldn't stand feeling lonely while living in the same house as you.'

And then she delivers the final blow.

'I just wanted to get away from you, Rohan. You drove me away.'

Distance

The very essence of romance is uncertainty.
Oscar Wilde

6
Rift

I am in bed but feel like I am falling. Like a huge chasm opened up under it and I am plummeting into it. It is as if the coordinates I had used to navigate life are no longer in place and I don't have a sense of what's going on any more. I am too shocked and shattered to respond. I don't know what to make of what Ira has just said. It's at odds with what I have always thought about our relationship.

For me it's been a fairy-tale love story of the new age: boy and girl become friends on the first day of college, fall in love and get married ten years later. Yes, it soon becomes a long-distance marriage, but I had taken that to be a sign of how deep our love is. How am I to accept now that it was all a facade, that beneath it we harbour the mundane resentment of an ordinary couple married for forty years? How am I to accept that I was such a lousy husband that she could not bear to be with me?

It doesn't add up. How strong is the foundation of our marriage after all?

'Hello? *Hello?*' Ira says, and I realize I haven't said anything for a long time. Should I fight back? Should I blame her for all that I hold against her? Should I meekly accept every charge and say sorry? But she hangs up before I can do anything, and I decide to leave it at that, at least for now.

Momo has gone to sleep at the foot of the bed. I want to kick him for triggering the whole fight—our first since … Earlier I would have said 'since Ira went to New York'. Now I complete the sentence with 'since she walked out on me'. Is that what it is, really? The truth is I'm not new to her temper. For all the things I love about her, she is a volatile person with a sharp tongue and I don't want to take what she says at face value.

It's six o'clock. I'm not able to go back to sleep. In fact, I'm unable to think of anything other than Ira. I wonder if she'll be able to focus on her assignment and submit it on time. Or would she be sitting in the library, upset and crying? I consider calling her back just to check on her but realize it may do more harm than good. Ira usually takes a few days to calm down, and calling her back in this state might start off another fight. I try to distract myself. I think of calling Yusuf. If he is on the night shift, he might be awake. But I check his Last Seen on WhatsApp—11.55 p.m. He must have been on the afternoon shift. And before I know it, I drift off to sleep.

I wake up at eleven. I sit up with a start in bed and realize I must have slept through Shobha's ringing of the doorbell. There's no missed call or text from Ira. I know she can be like that when we are fighting. So I try not to make too much of it. I want to speak to her. But it must be past midnight there, and the only thing she likes less than being disturbed in the middle of her work is being disturbed in the middle of the night.

I think of all those times she had asked me to get a job which wouldn't involve me reaching home at one, entering the house stealthily like an intruder and scaring her while she was asleep. I gave her a fright every day, she would tell me, and then she wouldn't be able to go back to sleep for an hour. But I had refused, saying I was doing well at work and was on the brink of a promotion. Ira was a light sleeper, and perhaps I did not take her problem seriously. Suddenly I miss her badly and want her in bed next to me so that I can watch her sleep. If it were not for the long distance, I'm sure we would have resolved the fight already.

I am distracted all day. There are few places more alive than a newsroom: editors quietly poring over the day's paper to look for mistakes, reporters speaking loudly on the phone as they try to get a quote from the police commissioner or home secretary or someone important, and news playing uninterruptedly on the TV screens of our vast floor even though nobody is really listening. I had hoped all the activity would help me take my mind off Ira, but it doesn't. I'm only waiting for it to be six-thirty so that it's eight in New York and she is awake.

The phone rings for a long time when I call her. The evening editorial meeting with the editor-in-chief has just got over, but it will be followed by a separate page one meeting with Maran, the resident editor, to freeze our line-up for the evening and begin work in all earnest. But I'm out in the corridor, having decided simply to say, 'It was urgent,' if I'm pulled up for skipping the meeting. I'm wondering if Ira is still sleeping or deliberately avoiding my call, when she answers and says, 'Hello.' She doesn't sound like I have woken her up.

'Hey,' I say, relieved that she did not ignore my call. Having spent the entire day waiting to talk to her, I'm strangely tongue-tied. 'Did you manage to submit your assignment on time?'

'No.'

'No?'

'No, I haven't. The rest of the class did. I'll get an F.'

I feel a stab of guilt. 'Come on. Can't you ask your professor for an extension?'

'There are other submissions I'm late for.'

We stay silent for some time. Reporters are arriving to file their stories after a day's work in the field. The editors who bring out the early edition are leaving. They all look at me curiously. I wonder what they can tell.

'Listen, I'm sorry, okay?' I say. 'I shouldn't have shouted at you or come in the way of your work. But it's wrong of you to think that I don't take your work seriously. I'm super proud of you. You're in a city that the world only dreams of visiting once in their lifetime. Of course I'm proud of you.'

'Rohan, I know you still don't understand. I know you still think it's one of my tantrums. It's not. I don't want to go over it again. At least not now. I'm not saying this to hurt you. But I want you to understand how desperate I must have been to have done what I did.'

'No, I don't get it.' My voice is rising. 'What do you want me to make of it? What has gone so horribly wrong? And even if something had, why did you leave without talking to me about any of this?'

'I did. You weren't listening.'

'What do you mean?'

'The fact that you don't remember shows you didn't take me seriously, Rohan. If you weren't listening then, there's no point now. I have a lot of work to do.'

'Fine.' I cut the call without waiting for her to react. I immediately regret it and think of calling her back, but I know she won't answer this time. It's anyway getting late and I need to be at my desk.

'Where were you?' Tanuj asks me as I sit down. 'Maran was asking about you in the meeting. I didn't know what to tell him.'

I shrug and say without looking at him, 'On the phone.'

He must have picked up on something in my voice. He doesn't say anything further. He doesn't probe, but even if he had, I wouldn't have minded. 'I've emailed the line-up for today,' he says, looking straight at his computer screen. 'We have an early deadline. There's some sort of special ad on the front page which they need to paste manually after the paper is printed.'

'All right.'

Five minutes later, he tags me on a funny dog video on Instagram with the message: 'Since these always cheer you up.'

*

I get off work early on Christmas Eve. Several of my colleagues, including Tanuj and Alisha, are going to Sacred Heart Cathedral, Delhi's biggest church. They ask me to join. I had anyway planned on going, but alone. I don't feel up to going with the rest. I turn down their offer, allow their cab a head start and then decide to walk to the cathedral, which is not too far from our office. The brightly lit grounds of the church are usually so crowded on Christmas Eve, and the visitors so immersed in the festivities, that I figure the others will never spot me dawdling by myself.

Ira and I had gone to Sacred Heart last year. All the roads converging at the GPO roundabout were so chock-a-block that we had to park the car ahead of Bangla Sahib and walk back. It had been unexpectedly cold and my teeth were chattering. I had wondered if it was wise to have come, especially since neither of us was religious. But, despite the crowd, it had felt nice being part of the carnival atmosphere. We had sat by ourselves at the back, right through the mass up to one-thirty, when I had started dozing off and we had decided to leave.

This time I sit in the same spot as last year. I stare vacantly at the priest in the distance delivering the sermon and, without knowing it, I pray a little. I don't intend staying for too long. I just want to keep up the tradition Ira and I had started—convert something we had done just once into an established ritual. But when I get up and turn around to leave, I catch sight of my team milling about. Alisha sees me. She looks like she is about to call out, but hesitates for a moment and then drags the rest in a different direction before they can spot me. I'm grateful for her thoughtfulness.

The next day I take a picture of Momo looking grumpy in a Santa Claus hat I bought outside the church. Using Photoshop I write 'Merry Christmas from Ira & Rohan' on it in a cursive font and post it on Facebook, tagging Ira. It's the first thing I have posted since she and I fought. As usual, I get scores of comments and likes within minutes, but there's nothing from her.

It's eleven in the morning, I haven't brushed my teeth or shaved, and I haven't had breakfast, which is going cold in the kitchen. Instead, I slam my laptop shut and go back to sleep, the thick rajai pulled over my head. My phone rings around lunch time and I wake up hoping it's Ira. It's Ira's mother.

'Merry Christmas, Rohan,' she says.

'Merry Christmas, Mummy.'

'Are you sick?'

'No, no. I just woke up actually.'

'At one?'

'Yes, got back late from the midnight mass.'

'Good you went. It must be really cold in Delhi, right? Are you sure you are not sick?'

'Yes. All well, all well.'

'And how are things? What did Ira send you for Christmas?'

59

That's when it occurs to me she hasn't sent me anything. 'Nothing so far. Maybe the mail is slow because of the holidays. Anyway, there's no need for us to be formal with each other.'

'It's not a formality. It's your first Christmas away from each other. Did yours reach her?'

'Mine what?'

'Your gift. You sent her something, didn't you?'

'Yes, of course.' I realize I haven't sent her anything either, and I lie. 'She hasn't mentioned it, so I figure it hasn't reached yet. And what's special at home today?'

'I am baking a cake. Daddy is making prawn curry and rice.' By the time I hang up after the conversation drags for a while, the taste of the food I won't have is on my tongue and I skip lunch too.

The parcel arrives in the afternoon and I know Ira didn't forget. Ira never forgets. It's a pineapple upside down cake. Of course, she hasn't made it herself, like the one she baked last year. She has had it sent from Potbelly, her favourite restaurant here. But I know she chose it to stand in for her. She calls half an hour later.

'Merry Christmas.' There is a soft edge to her voice and I am transported back to all the times my body would melt under her kisses and caresses. I feel my being seeping into the bed as I close my eyes.

'Merry Christmas. Thanks for the cake.'

'You got it?'

I am cold with anticipation as if she were in bed next to me, closing her mouth over my ear—the sound of the ocean in dry Delhi. 'Yes ... Ira?'

'Yes?'

'Let's not fight. I don't feel good about it. It's been such a sad month. It's Christmas and I haven't eaten anything all day. I won't have the cake till you tell me we are good.'

'Don't be this way. It's not a fight. I don't want to upset you but you need to make an effort to understand.'

'I'll work towards undoing all of it. Just come back.'

'How? If you don't know what it is that needs fixing?'

'You tell me and I'll fix it.'

'It doesn't work that way. Anyway, I don't want to talk about this. What have you sent me?'

I consider lying and then sending her something on Amazon using one-day delivery. But I don't want to lie. 'Nothing,' I say. 'I'm sorry I forgot. I'll make up for it. Tell me something you really need. I want to give you something that'll be useful.'

'Unlike the cake?'

'That's not what I meant. You know that.'

'Just stop, Rohan. The whole country has shut down. Nothing will be delivered for another ten days.' She takes a long pause as if to gather her thoughts. 'That's not even the point,' she says. 'I loved you for ten years. How long are you going to play catch-up? When we got married, I thought you'd love me without me loving you first. Didn't I deserve it?' She takes a deep breath. 'What will you fix, Rohan? How will you fix it when you don't know what's broken? Fine, I'll tell you. I'm broken. And I know you don't have it in you to fix me—fix us. I came here to mend myself. At least let me be.'

And yet again we lapse into a brooding silence.

*

The next week passes without any contact between me and Ira. I decide to keep myself occupied with other things. I start leaving for work early. This means that the first couple of days, Alisha and I don't meet in the cafeteria for tea as our timings differ. But, on the fourth day, I see her walking up to me out of the corner of my eye as I sit at a table with an empty cup, lost in thought.

'I thought you had gotten over tea,' she says with a smile as she pulls up a chair and sits next to me.

'Could one ever?' I smile back, realizing she has altered her routine too, and I feel glad for her company.

My section of the office is empty when I reach at two-thirty. The editors start arriving only around four. Until then I go through the front pages of our rival newspapers to see how we compare. I look out for stories we may have missed and study the display the others have given them. I go through the wires to catch up on the news for the day. I haven't been asked to, but I put together the important stories from different agencies and pass them on to the team which brings out the early edition that goes to the states around Delhi. I like this time I have to myself. Being entirely focused on work helps me take my mind off Ira.

We have an early deadline on New Year's Eve. We have been asked to be in office by three, but I reach at one-thirty. Around two, I'm finishing the sandwich I had ordered from the canteen when Maran calls out and asks me to meet him in his room.

'Sit, sit, Rohan,' he says. The news is playing in the background and he looks relaxed. It's the last day of the year after all. 'How are things?'

'Going well,' I say tentatively.

'Just wanted to chat with you.'

It's difficult to say what I have been called for. 'Am I in trouble?' I ask with a smile.

'No, no, of course not. Just that for the past week I've been observing that you come to work really early and stick around for a while after the edition has gone to press at night ... As I told you during your appraisal, we will be promoting you next year.'

'Um, thanks for the reassurance,' I say, unsure about where this is going.

'What I mean is you don't need to make an impression. You're past that stage. I know you're a hard worker.'

'What?' I'm taken aback. 'No, I'm not doing this to make an impression. Just to keep myself occupied.'

'Why, what happened? Listen, how *are* things with your wife—Isha, is it?'

'Ira. Things are well. Thanks for asking.' I cross my hands and remain seated in front of him with the stubborn look of someone who doesn't want to say more.

'Yes, all right,' he says. 'Get back to work then.'

That day I take my time with the stories assigned to me and give lousy headlines, though I have perfectly good alternatives written down in my notepad. But by the time we wind up, I think about Maran's words again and reason that I could take my mind off Ira in other ways too. After all, it is the last day of the year. Time for new beginnings.

'What's your plan for the evening?' I ask Tanuj as he is packing up to leave.

'For the night, you mean. It's almost ten. Nothing, will go home and get some sleep.'

'Really?'

'Because it's the thirty-first? I'm boring that way,' he says with a smile. 'I don't like partying. At most I'll start reading a new book perhaps. I was thinking of Amy Poehler's *Yes Please*. I hear it's good.'

'I think I'm a little bit in love with her. Have you seen her show?'

'*Parks and Rec*? No, I meant to download it but didn't get around to it somehow.'

'I have it. Do you want to come over? I think I've some Old Monk left too.'

Tanuj looks like he really just wants to go home and sleep. But he looks over my shoulder at something behind me. I turn around and see it's Maran. I don't know what has transpired between the two, but Tanuj agrees. 'Sure, it'll be great. But there's another thing you should know about me.'

I look at him curiously.

'I don't drink either,' he laughs.

As we reach home and I turn on the lights, I realize it's the first time I'm having a guest over in the four months since Ira left. Momo has thankfully not ripped open the sofa or anything like that and the house is presentable. I change, hand Tanuj a spare set of clothes and go to the kitchen to prepare a peg for me and fill a glass of Coke for him as he connects his hard drive to my TV. Instead of *Parks and Recreation*, he suggests we watch an old crime comedy—*The Smell of Fear* in the Naked Gun series starring Leslie Nielsen. I haven't heard of the film but I agree. As I enter the bedroom, he shushes me and asks me to take a photo of him. Momo has snuggled up to him and gone to sleep with his head in his lap. I take the photo, rather amused.

'I didn't know dogs would take to me this easily,' he says. 'Never interacted with one before.'

'Momo was never faithful,' I say as I hand him his glass and turn off the lights.

As the film starts and I take small swigs of the rum, I'm surprised by how funny the film is. Its high point is a hilarious sex scene, which shows, as a soft, romantic song plays in the background, a montage of shots that are euphemisms for the act—a flower opening, a sausage being inserted into a long piece of bread, a performer shooting out of a cannon in a circus, a train roaring into a tunnel, an oil rig pounding the earth, followed by oil spurting out of the ground, a shell shooting out of a submarine, water bursting through a dam, crackers exploding in the sky and a basketball player dropping a ball through a hoop. But I don't think I stay up through the entire film. I have had too much to drink.

I am superstitious about what I do at midnight on the thirty-first of December, because I feel it sets the tone for the rest of the year. But, in spite of that, I don't try and stay up until midnight to call and wish Ira. With more than twenty minutes to twelve, I doze off or pass out—I'm not sure. Either way, I sleep with the knowledge that this is the best time I've had in months.

7
Influence

My resolution for the new year is to find a new role model. For years, Ira has been the only person I have looked up to and tried to be like, so much so that I don't remember now which likes and dislikes of mine are my own and which ones I've acquired from her. We started at a point of convergence—we both loved to read, were on the same side of political divides and were idealists who thought we'd become journalists to change the world. But then our interests started to diverge. I stayed in the field I had chosen while she decided to return to academics. Her interests became intellectual while mine remained pragmatic, almost pedestrian.

To be honest, we reached a point where I put up with things I didn't exactly enjoy just so I had her approval— like going to see an art opening on my off days instead of staying home, or helping her in the kitchen on days Shobha didn't turn up instead of ordering in from the local dhaba. I suppose it comes with being married. You do what your spouse likes so that you're in it together. But there are times when you don't want to keep up.

Now, I begin to admit to myself that I like white wine, not red; post rock, not classical music; *Friends* over *Seinfeld*; that I don't get magic realism and can't appreciate Rushdie and Marquez and Pamuk though I can't get enough of Tolkien and Rowling. I need a new role model—someone I can identify with, observe and emulate. Someone like a life coach. And before I know it, Tanuj becomes that person.

Tanuj and I had always got along well since the time I joined the *Estate*, but it's only now, as I make an effort to get to know people other than Ira, that I realize how much he and I have in common. We come from a similar middle-class Bombay background and stick out for our quiet, hard-nosed approach to work in a brash profession where people are constantly trying to pull each other down. If anything, he's the more sorted one. We are the same age but he is already two rungs above me. Which also means he earns more than me, but I try not to think of that. He is Maran's favourite; the equanimity with which he can handle the lead story on the front page changing half an hour before deadline on a breaking-news night is hard to find. And he is that rare desk hand reporters actually like.

In the time we have every day before the evening meeting, I try to draw Tanuj out of the newsroom and pick his brains during walks around the building about how he has come so far in his career in such a short span of time. I discover that he does not think of work as just editing stories and building a rapport with the seniors. In his spare time, he meets editors and journalists from other papers and magazines. He doesn't do it to consciously build a network or increase his odds of getting better job offers—even if that is the intention. He does it naturally. He meets them at book clubs, cultural events or on jaunts around town to discover good places to eat.

On the other hand, I had all along thought of my job as a means to make just enough money to get by every month while my focus was either on completing my master's or convincing Ira's parents to let us marry. Now I realize that being hard at work in a corner of the office isn't going to get me anywhere. All that Tanuj does is as much a part of shaping one's career as crossing the t's and dotting the i's in the stories I edit.

I decide I want to be more like him and start with the superficial things. From floaters, jeans and round-neck T-shirts, I switch to black formal shoes, cotton trousers and full-sleeve shirts, tucked in. And I can tell the difference immediately. Not only do the reporters take me seriously but I myself do too. My approach to those around me becomes more professional and I feel more engaged with my work.

There's one problem, though. The young interns do not turn around to take a second look at me when I'm walking by. They do that for Tanuj. I can see their eyes linger on him and hear them giggle. And it's not just because they know I'm married while he's still single. I see myself in the glass door of the office gym one day and decide to follow Tanuj in there for an hour every afternoon before work.

The first time we stand before the mirror in the changing room does not do good things to my self-esteem. Tanuj's clean physique is enviable. He has the body of a swimmer without the bulk of a gym junkie, while on my puny frame I can only see scraggly hair and loose skin. It's not like I'm seeing myself like this for the first time, or that Ira has never made fun of my love handles. But I've never before measured myself against a benchmark. I quickly put on my gym clothes and scoot out, hoping Tanuj did not see what I did.

I'm a little unsure of what I can do without exposing my rookie status. I've been on a treadmill before, so I go for that. But just five minutes on it, even at a speed of 5.0 and at zero incline, and I'm gasping for breath through my mouth. Tanuj, on the one next to me, has headphones over his ears, and I can hear faint strains of 'Zinda' from Bhaag Milkha Bhaag as he runs faster and faster at an increasing incline and continues to breathe normally. If I were in high school, I would have been ragged and molested all the way out of the gym. Thankfully, Tanuj is more sympathetic to my plight and realizes I might need some help. But even he can't stop himself from laughing when I slowly lift my knees and stomach off the floor during my first push-up, tentatively look like I'll dive back to complete at least one, and then fall flat.

Next, he goes for the 15 kg weights. He sees me reach for the 5 kg ones and says, 'Those are for wo—' but it's too late. I've already picked them up and am grinning.

It's hard to keep up with Tanuj as he rests his hand on his knee and raises the dumbbell to his chin, or when he stands up, holds one in each hand, and raises them first to his shoulders and then over his head. He has clearly been doing this for a long time. Not only do I manage to lift the weights only ten times against his twenty, but I'm also doing it all wrong. He notices that I'm bending my arms at an odd angle and helps me hold them tighter. I feel the pull in my muscles but persevere.

'It's okay, you know,' he says encouragingly. 'You don't have to kill yourself on your first day.'

'It's—high—time,' I groan as he props up my elbows with his hands so I can complete a decent number.

'I'll tell you the same thing my first gym instructor once told me,' he says. 'Imagine there is a party and you're walking into a big hall with your girl. All eyes will be on the two of you as you make an entrance. She'll be a little shy and will hold on to you for reassurance. Now think which part of your body she will hold and focus on that. Do weights and push-ups if you see her holding your arm. Pull-ups if you see her placing her hand on your shoulder in a ballroom dance. Crunches if you see her putting her arm around your waist.'

It's sensible advice, no doubt, but I cannot see myself walking into a room with any woman in the foreseeable future, least of all Ira. And I cannot for the life of me imagine her holding on to me shyly. So I just soldier on without much motivation. Despite the agony and the trauma of not having functional limbs for the next one week, I do everything Tanuj does: squats, half-squats, one-legged hops and forward kicks, succumbing finally to reverse crunches. I end up merely sitting on a bench and studying him as he lies down and raises his legs perpendicular to the floor.

*

'Have you been working out?' Alisha asks as I sit in the chair opposite her. We are at a table on the terrace of Diggin, a new place opposite Gargi College. It's the end of January and the sun is out after a long time.

Alisha was shocked when I mentioned to her one day while driving past the cafe that I haven't been here yet. 'It's the best thing about our neighbourhood right now,' she had said and offered to treat me. I had looked it up on Zomato and, taken in by its wooden flooring, the low-hanging lamps, the tree mural, the spacious seating and the cost for two of Rs 1,350, agreed gladly.

'Yes,' I say with a smile. 'Can you tell?'

'Your shoulders did suddenly look slightly broader than usual,' she says. 'They have been for a few days actually, but I thought it was just something to do with the jackets you were wearing. Today you are only wearing a shirt and I still got the impression, so asked.'

I can't tell for sure but I think I'm blushing. It'll be embarrassing if she found out, so I hold the menu card in front of my face. 'Thanks,' I say from behind it, 'for the compliment. And for the treat. You didn't need to really.'

'After all the times you paid for my tea in office, this is the least I could do,' she says. 'In addition to telling the women in my team what a gentleman you are. They say it's a pity you are married.'

I look up to see if she is flattering me or pulling my leg. But I can only see a poker face. I clear my throat and ask, 'What would you suggest we have?'

We order crispy zucchini fries, a chicken and jalapeno pizza and lamb lasagne. For dessert we have chocolate mud pie. It is without doubt the best food I have had in months. On my salary, and having to pay the EMIs on the loan I have taken for Ira, eating out had until today meant momos at a Chinese food cart near my place or good but cheap food in Old Delhi with Tanuj. Diggin's is a taste I had forgotten I knew.

'Such a gentleman,' she says again as I hold open the door of the car for her.

'Not that again!' I say, coming around and getting into the driver's seat.

'What? You sound like it's a bad word.'

'It *is* if you think about it. Sounds like I'm so harmless that women won't take me seriously. That's what it is. It's a cover for not taking note of me.'

'It's not. You don't know what a rare breed you are. Women die to be around men they aren't threatened by.'

'And what a world of good does it do me? I'm still the one without a wife. I tell you what,' I say, looking directly at her and smiling so that she knows I'm joking, 'I've had enough of this. I'm going to go out there and have a solid, sordid, torrid extra-marital affair.'

She laughs loudly. 'See now you're caught in a Catch-22 situation. You come across as harmless and non-threatening is why women are attracted to you. But they'll be turned off the minute you decide to act on it.'

'Just speak for yourself.'

'Me? I do find you gentlemanly, non-threatening, harmless and attractive. But sadly I'm off men. It'll be a while before I lick the wounds of my break-up.'

'Oh, damn it,' I say dramatically and pretend to sulk for the rest of the commute.

Tanuj gives me a quizzical look as I sit in my chair after I have reached office and Alisha has gone off to her section. I shrug and say, 'What's up? What's the ad situation like?'

'Half page. We can all relax and go home at ten.'

'Yeah, right. You know well a half page means the lead will keep changing.'

'Forget that,' he says, moving on to more pressing matters. 'I meant to ask you, have you heard of Kunzum Travel Cafe?'

'The one in Hauz Khas? Yes. Why?'

'They have organized a road trip to Alwar and back next-to-next Sunday. All groups have to get their own cars and we follow the lead vehicle to the Hill Fort Kesroli heritage hotel, where we have lunch and come back. I'll send you the email. The hotel's got splendid green views from its ramparts. I was supposed to go with some friends from ToI but they've backed out. Will you come? You'll have to drive, though. I'm not sure I can keep up with the other guys.'

I jump at the opportunity and agree readily. I'm always up for a good long drive. When I failed my driving test ten years ago, it stung me so badly that I set my mind on not just learning the skill but mastering the art. I practised night after night with Appa until I imbibed his fine touch. So, now when I drive, it's about more than just getting from point A to point B. It's liberating. It's about rising above my limitations. When I drive, all that is inessential falls away and I only commune with my car and the road ahead. It's like the car is an extension of me. I feel so completely in control that I enter a space of infinite possibilities. It may sound contradictory but it isn't really. It's like imagination. When you are truly in control of it, you can make anything happen.

8
Travellers

Tanuj stays the night at my place. We have to meet the Kunzum group in Gurgaon at seven on what will be a cold February morning, and it would have been a long commute for him just to get to Shahpur Jat from Noida, where he lives. The alarm goes off at five-thirty. We get out of bed groggily and reluctantly. While he has a quick shower, I prepare coffee and butter toast; he feeds Momo as I get dressed, and we're good to go at six-fifteen.

Tanuj connects his phone to the music player, and we listen to Frank Sinatra's 'Come Fly with Me', which is apt as we zip through the fog on empty flyovers, and it does feel like we are gliding through clouds. It's quite chilly in Gurgaon. We are among the first to reach the meeting point—MGF Mall. The organizers of the road trip arrive and start distributing hot tea in paper cups as they ask us to fill out our details on a sheet of paper. Since most people who are part of the trip don't know each other, they also pass around stickers on which we have to write our names and put on our chests.

As more arrive, Tanuj goes around to make introductions while I stay by my car and consent to having a poster pasted on its bonnet. It says, 'Club Kunzum: We Travel. What Do You Do?' under line sketches of the seven wonders of the world. Most of our fellow travellers are in Renault Dusters or BMWs or Mahindra Thars. The adventurous of the lot turn up on Bullets. Their pillion riders have video cameras mounted on selfie sticks, which I presume they intend to use to shoot us when in motion.

We leave at seven-thirty. Eighteen cars, all with the Kunzum posters on their doors and bonnets, driving in a formation on the highway make for quite a sight. We were told not to get ahead of the designated first car or fall behind the designated last one in the line. The latter wouldn't be a problem, I had assured Tanuj; I would never deign to fall behind just because we're the only ones in a hatchback. Soon enough, I'm overtaking trucks and staying at the head of the line, just behind the lead vehicle.

I note in passing that it has a Punjab registration number. It makes me think of another road trip that Tanuj and I had planned but which wasn't meant to be. In January, we had decided to drive across Punjab to see the Golden Temple for the first time. There was no patch-up in sight with Ira, and I was really looking forward to the five-hundred-kilometre-long drive to clear my head. But Tanuj had backed out at the last minute, citing too much work. There's no patch-up in sight even now; Ira and I haven't spoken for weeks. But I on my part finally decided it was better to sidestep the fight than to let it pull me down. And I'm glad that at least this road trip to Alwar did materialize.

'I'm forgiven for Amritsar, I hope?' Tanuj says, putting on his sunglasses once the sun is finally out.

'Yes, of course,' I say casually, even though I had been quite upset back then when he had cancelled, and am a little spooked now that he is able to read my mind like this.

'But was it work, really, because of which you cancelled? I work in the same office, you know, and I'm aware our job doesn't require us to take work home.'

'Smart boy. Okay, it was work, but not related to office. Something personal came up. Will tell you about it some other time.' I turn my mind back to the road.

An hour into the drive, the national highway is still clear but I'm not trying to be at the head of the line any more. We cruise along at a steady speed of eighty. Once in a while, one of the Bullets overtakes us and we smile and wave at the cameras. As we drive past mustard fields, Tanuj, who generally uses puns as a manner of speaking, asks me, 'What do you call sarson da saag that's been left in the fridge for two days?' I have known him long enough to give the standard response: 'What?' 'Parson da saag,' he replies and I laugh grudgingly.

By now it's bright and sunny. I roll down the window and let the strong wind toss my hair up and whip my face. It's almost like I'm driving on auto-pilot. Tanuj and I talk about Sinatra and Sigur Ros and I make him listen to '*Hoppipolla*'. I tell him about Yusuf and how he had introduced me to the happiest song I've ever heard. We discuss our colleagues and discover that there are a lot of common people we want to bitch about—the woman who heads the education supplement and keeps screaming at her team, the rich girls on the nation desk who only ever talk about their spa and salon visits, and the new guy on the web desk who has never been spotted doing any work. I suggest to Tanuj that we go to a different state bhavan canteen every so often as we both like to explore new places to eat.

He asks me if I would like to become a member of a new book club he has joined. 'We meet on Sunday afternoons. You've got to talk about one book that you've read and carry one to lend to anyone who might be interested.'

'Sounds fun. Where do you guys meet?'

'It's usually at the home of one of the members. By default that means somewhere in south Delhi, so shouldn't be a problem for you. They asked me if I'd like to host one of our meets but I doubt if anyone will be willing to come all the way to Greater Noida on a Sunday afternoon.'

'You stay in Noida, don't you?'

'Yes, but I'll be moving out soon.'

'Why Greater Noida? Why not someplace closer to Delhi?'

'I've bought a flat there, actually. Couldn't have afforded one in Delhi!'

'You've *what*!' The thought had never crossed my mind that anybody my age in my profession could be in a position to even make the down payment on a flat.

'It's in an under-construction property in the back of beyond. I doubt if I'll be able to go to state bhavans and book club meets once I've moved there.'

'Man, how much money *do* you make?' I ask baldly.

He laughs and says, 'It's on a loan, of course.'

'Still, you'll be paying your own EMIs, right? I don't think I'm in a position to do even that.'

'It's not about the income but the savings. Ever since I moved to Delhi, I've only lived in flats whose rent was never more than ten grand and always shared it with at least two other guys. I knew I had to buy a house before I turn thirty, even if it's somewhere far.' I feel small again, never having given serious thought to money matters.

We are properly satiated by the time we reach Hill Fort Kesroli around noon. It's a heritage property turned into a hotel with a sky-blue swimming pool. It is surrounded on all sides by open green fields, which stretch for miles and make for a great backdrop for photos. Over lunch we get to know our fellow travel enthusiasts. Tanuj and I share a table with a retired army general, who is a regular on Kunzum trips. He tells us his children are settled abroad and his wife passed away last year. Since then, he doesn't like to be home because it reminds him too much of her, and so he wakes up every Sunday morning, gets behind the wheel and hits the road without deciding where he wants to go. I tell him how much I identify with him but can't do what he does because, unlike the rest of the world, I have an office to attend even on Sundays. Post lunch, people start leaving one by one; we aren't going to return to Delhi in one formation the way we had come. So, after chatting with a few people in the group who run homestays in quiet hilly towns around Delhi we haven't heard of, Tanuj and I leave too.

He volunteers to drive on the way back since there aren't other cars we have to keep up with. We stray off the highway once but turn back without losing much time after asking for directions. The sky darkens and we fall silent as he strains his eyes against the glare of the high beams of the headlights of the vehicles coming from the opposite direction, and I stare out the window, thinking of Ira and the retired general's words.

The memory of his dead wife drives him out of his home, I drove Ira out of ours and now the bitterness that hangs in the air does the same to me. Looking at the dark swathes of fields I could have been driving past with Ira at a different time in our lives, I wonder if there is a definite amount of love within us, and what happens when its taker no longer wishes to take. What happens when a part of your soul attached to someone for a long time comes loose?

I tend to brood every time a holiday is about to come to an end, so I ask Tanuj if he wants me to drive. I don't tell him this, but I'd like to be behind the wheel again just to take my mind off unpleasant thoughts. But he refuses. I doze off after a while. When I wake up, I find we are in Delhi.

'You drove the whole distance?' I say, rubbing my eyes and sounding a little surprised.

'I'm not that bad, you know.'

'Well, clearly you aren't. How else would I have slept peacefully for two hours?'

'Thanks, but I can't be as good as you. So please take the wheel now. My bum has gone numb.'

Half an hour later, I drive into the lane outside Hauz Khas metro station. Tanuj says he'll take a train from here to Noida. 'So on a scale of one to ten, how will you rate the trip?' he asks, unfastening the seat belt. The movie buff that he is, Tanuj likes to review films in his free time, and his impulse to rate often targets other mundane things as well.

Despite the depressing thoughts right before I dozed off, I know this drive was exactly the change I had needed. 'Um, nine,' I say.

He peels the sticker with his name on it off his chest and sticks it in the top left corner of the windshield. 'I'm not walking into a metro station with that on. What if some hot girl decides to stalk me?' he says in a tone that conveys he would very much like that to happen. Then he steps out and climbs down the stairs into the subway.

*

The next day, I'm waiting for Alisha outside her place in the afternoon when I see her walking in my direction. She had texted me an hour ago to say she wasn't up to taking the metro today and ask if she could hitch a ride with me to office. I had assumed she was feeling unwell and readily agreed, but I see the real reason now. She is wearing black stilettos, matching winter stockings and a pencil skirt, and a blood red top. I'm seeing her after a week, but I know she's objectively looking different. I don't want her to think I'm ogling, so I look away.

'What happened?' she asks as she gets in the car.

I didn't realize the grin on my face was discernible. 'You're looking different today,' I mumble. 'Nice different. I mean, I've only ever seen you in jeans and T-shirts, so this is, you know, a considerable change.'

As I turn on the engine and look at the traffic ahead, she smiles and says, as if she is wondering if I'm flirting with her, 'Thank you. I wanted to try a new look for my birthday.'

'It's your birthday today?' I turn to her and seem guilty for not knowing, while keeping an eye on the road at the same time.

'Twenty-fifth.'

'I'm kicking myself. I hope you know that.'

'It's all right.' She adds after a pause, 'You're looking different too.'

'You're just saying it now.' I hope I'm not visibly blushing.

'No, I mean it. You've settled into your new wardrobe. And the beard suits you. You've lost some of that paunch too!' I grow conscious of the middle portion of my body as I sense her eyes on it, but she sounds casual.

'Thanks,' I say. 'I haven't attempted a new look since kindergarten. It was high time. And it's good to know all that time I'm spending in the gym with Tanuj is making a difference.'

'Absolutely.'

'And how was home? Why didn't you extend your stay by a day and celebrate your birthday there?'

'Oh, Jaipur is just like being in Delhi. It was all right. And I wanted to be around friends for my birthday. But while I was there, I decided I have to get back into the dating circuit. I'm not off men any more.'

I almost brake instead of accelerating as the traffic clears. She looks at me weirdly, then says, 'Jaipur does that to me. Half the men you meet in Delhi newsrooms don't bathe, shave or have a sense of dressing. One quarter are mamma's boys or gay and the straight quarter are round. One almost forgets the strapping men you get to see in Jaipur. *Men* men—you know what I mean?'

I laugh and say, 'No, I don't. Give me an example. Am I a strapping *man* man?'

'No, I'm not talking about you. I'm not talking about anyone in office. All the men in office are so … *blah*!'

I laugh. 'Are you aware of all the incorrect things you're saying right now?'

'Well, I don't believe in namby-pamby correctness … Of course, what I say has to stay inside this car.'

I laugh louder. 'My car is a confessional?'

'Yes, that's exactly what it is.'

'Okay, maybe I should also confess a few things then.'

'Maybe you should,' she says encouragingly, but then we fall silent, both of us perhaps trying to decide if I meant what I said or if I said it in jest. I am also unexpectedly gladdened by the piece of information she let slip: that she wanted to be around friends for her birthday. I don't know for sure if I fall in that category—and it's true we only have a dreadful evening in office ahead of us—but I feel happy in the presumption that I do. And it's best to keep your thoughts to yourself when you feel that kind of happiness.

9

Divorce

March begins with the retreating of winter. On Holi when I see Varun in shorts, drenched and smeared with colour from head to toe, dance drunkenly down the street with his friends, I know the season is finally over. One by one I get Shobha to wash all the woollens, fold them, pack them in a suitcase and stow them away in the kitchen loft. Within a few weeks it will be hard to remember there was recently a time when I did not need to switch on the fans in the house or when I would shiver merely at the thought of being doused in cold water. Which is why I am glad that what happens in Alisha's house one morning happens only at the end of winter.

She sounds frantic and almost on the verge of tears on the phone. She is also incoherent. I am not able to figure out much other than that she is desperately calling me over. I sense trouble and rush downstairs to get into the car. I quickly cut through the traffic as rashly as I can and reach her place in ten minutes. When she opens the door, she looks frazzled, kajal running down her eyes, and she is soaked to the bone. Behind her I see a two-inch-high puddle advancing towards the door.

'The tap in the kitchen just came off,' she says, 'and I can't make the water stop.'

As she closes the door, I wade and reach the kitchen, which is at the end of a long corridor. Water is gushing out of where the tap had been. The walls are wet too. I figure that she must have tried to put the tap back on in vain, causing the water to spray all around. Plastic bags and old rags are strewn on the kitchen platform. She must have attempted to stuff those into the pipe, but again in vain. I try to do the same—with the same result.

'Do you have a screwdriver or a wrench?' I ask, almost certain she is going to say no. These are not tools you find in the house of a single woman. But she runs into her bedroom and comes back with pliers.

'This is all I can find,' she says.

'Perfect,' I say. I pick up one of the longer pieces of cloth off the platform and try to drive it into the pipe. It takes me five minutes but finally the water stops.

'I can't believe you managed it,' she says with a sense of relief. 'I've never felt so helpless before.'

'Glad I could help. What happened exactly?'

'I was making breakfast when I noticed water dripping from the tap even though it was shut. I tried slamming it down but it just came off. It's an old house, and the plumbing is poor. This kitchen doesn't have a valve I can use to turn off the supply either. I tried fixing the tap back on but got drenched.' She pauses and looks awkward. 'Let me quickly go in and change,' she says. 'But what about you?'

'It's not a problem. I'll stand in the sun in the balcony. I'll dry soon.'

Fifteen minutes later, I'm leaning over the railings and looking at the guards at the gate below who are eyeing me suspiciously when Alisha walks up from behind and hands me a steaming cup of coffee.

'Oh, thanks,' I say, gladly accepting it. 'What about all the water on the floor? We'll need to push it towards the bathroom so it drains.'

'It can wait.'

I instantly feel warm inside as I take swigs of the coffee. 'Not that I had a problem coming over—as I said, I'm glad I could help—but why didn't you just call the guards or a plumber?'

'It's not easy being a woman staying alone in Delhi, Rohan,' she says, the tips of her hair curling up with the steam from her mug. 'These men are guards only by profession. There have been nights when they have tried to enter my house claiming that they saw someone suspicious in the balcony. I don't feel safe around them. They asked you lots of questions on your way up, didn't they? I'm sure you don't face any such problems with your guards.'

I nod. As she pauses to outstare the guards still looking up, it occurs to me how different a woman's lived reality is from a man's and how little a man realizes it.

'There was no time to call a plumber from outside,' she continues. 'And if I had called the society plumber, the neighbours would have found out what happened. They anyway look at me weirdly and am sure talk behind my back. Now they would have blamed me for emptying the tank also. It is as all the neighbourhood aunties say— unattached women in India become the subject of loose talk rather easily.'

'Don't be too upset about what happened today,' I say, hoping I sound reassuring enough. 'Such things happen.'

'Oh no, I'm not upset. In fact, in a weird sort of way, I'm glad this happened. I think it's the sign I was looking for all these months.'

'What sign?'

'Okay, don't tell anyone. I have yet to discuss it with Maran. But I can't not tell you after all you've done for me today. I've decided to move back to Jaipur ... You remember you had asked me why I didn't stay back home for my birthday and I had said I wanted to spend the day with my friends? It was because I knew I won't be around them on my next birthday.'

I stare at her without saying anything. I've dried in the sun by now but feel like I've been doused with cold water once more.

'Don't tell me it's just because of the men there!' I say, trying to sound casual and funny.

She laughs a hollow laugh and says seriously, 'I think I've had enough of this life. I think I want to go back home. I had applied to a few places, and when I went to Jaipur last month, it was to appear for an interview at

ToI. They called me yesterday with an offer and I was debating with myself if it's really wise to move back just because I can't bear to live alone any more. If I'll be doing it for the right reasons. I was unsure but I think this incident was just the sign I needed. It's made making up my mind a lot easier.'

'Really? You're going to move cities because the tap in your kitchen broke?' I say, trying not to sound too grave.

'No, of course not,' she says with a straight face. 'I've moved cities all my life, but I had been asking myself what I'm doing here. I had come to Delhi because my boyfriend was here. It makes no sense for me to stay on now. I think I was holding on to a part of my old life, hoping that I might some day return to it. I need to face up to reality and accept that that's not happening. I need to make a clean break.'

She pauses to sip on the coffee. 'And it will be nice to be around my mum,' she says. 'You know, growing up, I didn't get much time with her. We moved countries so often, looking back it now feels like whatever time we did get with each other, I was too disoriented with the transition to really appreciate her. She's retired now and it will be nice to have her around—you know, do some spadework with her in our little garden.'

I stay silent. 'I know a lot of people think of me as this strong, independent person who's happy to be by herself. But, honestly, who ever wants that? Who wants to live a lonely, loveless life? At the end of the day, we all just want to be around the people we care for deeply. So to give you the short answer, yes, I've decided to accept the offer and move to Jaipur.'

Coffee mugs in hand, we silently look at the cars revving their engines and leaving for work, the children in uniform going off to school and vegetable vendors setting up their carts. At a different time in our lives, I had stood in a balcony like this alongside Ira.

'I'm sure you must miss Ira too,' Alisha says unexpectedly. 'You know, Rohan, I'm a fan of yours. I honestly do admire you a lot. It's so heartening to see that Ira is doing her own thing in New York and you here. Touch wood, you have such a healthy relationship. And one day she'll be back.'

The irony of it is just too much for me to bear and I look away.

*

As soon as we reach office, Alisha goes into Maran's room to put in her papers. Through the glass door, I see him look at her with a smile, which quickly turns into a frown. He picks up the phone and a minute later Alisha's immediate boss goes in too. They all talk animatedly. They obviously don't want her to leave, but I wonder what they can do if she wants to move back home. Throughout, Alisha remains seated in the chair, looking docile yet smiling. Maran picks up the phone a few more times and talks to someone in HR, I presume. The meeting drags on. It's not over even forty-five minutes later. When Tanuj arrives, he drops his bag in his chair and looks at me. 'What's happening?' he asks.

'Nothing. What made you late?'

'Come with me. I'll tell you,' he says and I reluctantly go with him downstairs. He looks mysterious and happy in an odd sort of way, not saying a word until we are out of the building through the back gate, have bought two cups of tea from a roadside vendor and are standing way out of earshot of our colleagues who are just arriving. I'm just starting to wonder if he too has got another job offer when he announces, 'I'm getting married.'

I'm stunned. I didn't even know he was dating. 'It all happened this morning,' he says, not noticing how shocked I look. 'The wedding is in May in Kolkata and you're the first person I'm inviting. You have to come!'

'Of course.' Remembering how to react, I give him a hug and say, 'Congratulations! But *who* is she? I'm bloody mad you didn't tell me you had a girlfriend but I'll pick that bone later.'

'No, no. It's an arranged marriage.' I'm all the more stunned by this. Given how free-spirited and independent he has always been, I never pegged him as the sort of guy who would get married, leave alone have an arranged marriage. I'm at a loss.

'Well, it's not exactly arranged,' he continues. 'In the sense it's not like our parents fixed us up. I knew her elder sister. We had worked together in Bombay. We got in touch a few weeks back and she told me they are looking for a guy for her younger sister. You know, one thing led to another, I cancelled our Amritsar trip and met Tanvi instead. It was serendipity, Rohan. There's no other word for it. My mum had made me meet so many girls but I just didn't feel any connection with them. But with Tanvi, the moment we met, I said to myself, "My search ends here." It really was serendipity.'

I smile. I had heard about things unfolding like this but never experienced it myself. Ira and I had been friends ten years before we got married.

'The very next day I told her sister that it was a yes from my side,' he continues. 'Tanvi took her time but she called me this morning to say that she liked me for my earnestness. She said I looked like the kind of person who would make her happy and she agreed. Phone calls were made between Bombay, Delhi and Kolkata and finally a date in May was fixed. It's all happening so quickly but I'm thrilled.'

Crushing his empty cup of tea and discarding it in a nearby bin, he says as we start walking back to office, 'I've bought a house, you know, I'm getting married now. It feels like I've arrived in life.'

*

At night, when I turn the key and open the door, everything looks so unfamiliar in the dark that I feel I've walked into someone else's house. As I look around, I realize this is not home. For twenty-two years of my life, entering home had meant entering a brightly lit drawing room where Amma would be setting the dining table for dinner and Appa would be reading the newspaper, folded twice, in the kitchen while keeping an eye on the milk on the stove. Then, for one glorious year after marriage, it had meant walking into a room with the lights turned out and watching Ira sleep. Home had always meant peace and quiet, never darkness and such disquiet.

After all the time I've spent on the periphery of others' lives, Momo makes me feel important by nuzzling my hand, asking for food. I don't turn on the lights. I sit down on the floor and stroke his back, feeling grateful for his presence. Brood as I may, I'm unable to wrap my head around what I'm feeling. I think it's anger at Ira for this overwhelming loneliness, in the face of which I find myself helpless. But I suspect it's something more and I'm not able to put my finger on it.

I take out my phone, its light filling up the room, and scroll down my contacts. I wonder whom to call, if at all. There's a tremendous force inside that makes me want to reach out, but to what or to whom I cannot tell. Suddenly when I look up, the walls feel closer than they are. I jump, pick up my car keys and leave.

Without any destination in mind, for an hour I drive around south Delhi. I drive through the dead lanes of Hauz Khas and Green Park, Safdarjung Enclave and R.K. Puram, looking up at the closed windows of Delhi's elite who have the money for all they need. I join the traffic of the trucks on the Ring Road and go in the opposite direction all the way to Kalkaji. I slow down to a crawl so that the guy behind starts honking, then I speed up so that my butt cheek is off the seat as my right leg holds the accelerator down. I don't know what I'm looking for or hoping to do. Perhaps to whip up a storm to take up all my mind space. I take a U-turn at Okhla and race myself back to Shahpur Jat. But when it's close to two and I'm nowhere near calm enough to go to bed, I call up Gaurav in a vague hope. He is awake.

'Come over,' he says, and I change course to go to JNU.

'Chandrabhaga, 221,' I roll down the window on the passenger's side and tell the guard at the gate. He eyes me suspiciously because it's so late. I wonder if he'll now make me call Gaurav and ask him who his hostel warden is in order to verify if he really is a student. But he waves me through after handing me a blue token.

'Hey roomie,' Gaurav says in his usual deep, hollow voice and gives me a hug as he opens the door of his hostel room. I know it makes me seem pathetic but I don't let go, despite his bristly chin digging into my shoulder.

'Had a bad day?' he asks, rubbing my back.

I finally let go. 'Yeah, sorta,' I say, looking into his eyes that are glazed as usual behind his Gandhi glasses.

'Okay, come. Let me pour you a drink.' The room is barely big enough for the two single beds and littered with unwashed clothes and empty packets of Haldiram's Mint Lachha. Mercifully, his roommate is out. Gaurav opens his cupboard and takes out a half-empty bottle of Old Monk. He retrieves a plastic cup from under his bed, pours some of the rum into it and adds some Coke. He already has his glass ready.

'Out with it. Girl trouble?' he asks.

'I'm not in college.'

'But you *are* married. Which is worse.'

I give him a wry smile and drink.

'How are things at work?'

'Swell. Everybody's life is set but mine.'

'Who everybody?'

'Everybody. People who talk of leaving jobs without so much as a thought. People who've got things figured out so right that they can buy homes and marry strangers and know they'll be happy. People sitting pretty in N-Y-C.'

'Ho, ho, back up. Did you and Ira have a fight?'

'No. Not today at least. Anyway, let's not talk about all this. Let's watch something.'

Gaurav decides to introduce me to *Breaking Bad*, which he claims will blow my mind. 'Since you don't smoke up, this is the second trippiest thing you can do,' he says. I agree; the show is gripping from the get-go. But having seen the forty-five-minute first episode once before, Gaurav sleeps off even as it runs on his laptop. And it's too depressing for me right now—not so much because of Walt's lung cancer but the bleak and barren Albuquerque landscape and the suffocating idea of the man as the provider of the family even if he's dying—so I turn it off and give in to the itch to call Ira.

'Hello?' Her voice is calm.

'Hi. What are you doing?'

'Nothing, meeting some friends for dinner later. Why? What time is it there?'

'Three-thirty.' She doesn't ask why I'm up so late.

'Are you online? We can video chat,' she says.

'No. Don't have wi-fi here.'

'Where are you?'

'Gaurav's room, JNU.' She doesn't ask why I'm here.

Silence.

'I'm upset,' I say.

'Why?'

'I don't know.'

Silence.

'Do you want to talk about it?' she asks.

'Do *you* want to talk about it?' I say.

Long pause.

'Yes, tell me what happened.'

'I don't know what I'm doing with my life.'

'In what sense?'

'Every sense. I have no career, no money, no marriage to speak of. What more do I say?'

'These things take time. Don't be upset.'

'That's what I had thought when we started living together. That now that we share the rent, we'll have some savings, now I can focus on my career, maybe think about buying a house. And look at me now. Half my salary goes in paying bills and the other half in paying EMIs.'

'Are you saying I am the reason for this?'

'I did not say that.'

'Then what are you saying?'

'I'm saying what I said. That I have no career, no money, no marriage.'

'You know, Rohan, I'm sick of this. You call to complain and say you're upset. But all you really want to do is blame me. Why not just do it directly?'

'Okay, maybe I do want to blame you. I've done so much for you and you can't even talk to me without fighting once. I moved to Delhi to be with you, took up a job so we could get married and what did you do? You flew off and left me alone here. Do you know how depressing it is to go home every night? I want to ask people if they'll hang out with me so I don't feel lonely, but I don't because it makes me feel like shit.'

'What do you want me to do, Rohan? Do you want me to be eternally grateful to you that you took a loan for me? Did I not give you all the money I made when I did have a job? I gave you *ten* years of my life. *Ten* years to get you to like me. And the moment we were married, it was like you didn't care. You were like this even then. You expected me to be grateful that you married me. You just didn't try to do anything to make me happy. You were never excited about celebrating festivals together—or going on a weekend holiday somewhere. Do you remember my first birthday after we got married? Do you remember not giving me any gift? Remember me being upset about it for twenty-one days straight? All you said was you wanted it to be something grand, that you were saving up for it. But couldn't you have given me something small—a greeting card, a letter? I didn't want something grand. I just wanted my husband to make me feel loved for a day. But you didn't care. Do you remember me crying about my job every night? You won't because you were never there. Because you were at work. So *what* exactly should I be grateful for, Rohan? That you loved me for one year to my ten and then gave up after the wedding?'

Long silence. Neither of us talks. I close my eyes, the phone over my ears. I don't know what to say. I want to disconnect the call and go to sleep and never wake up. I grit my teeth silently. I had done everything right. I thought I had. How was I to know that it would all eventually come to this?

'When did we become so resentful of each other, Ira?' I say, my eyes still shut. 'When did we become so bitter?'

'You need to answer that question. Because you made me this way.'

I summon the last reserves of calm and patience and fortitude. 'We'll be fine when you come back. It won't be like this again.'

'You only say these things. You only make promises you never keep. So many things you had promised when you proposed to me. "I will fill your life with happiness or die trying." That is what you had said to me. And look now what you've done.'

'It will be different this time.'

'I'm not even sure there's going to be a "this time".'

'What are you saying?'

'That I'm not even sure I want to come back. I think I want to cancel my return ticket and just stay here without a break for the second year.'

'You will do no such thing, Ira,' I say, my temper rising. I know she is perfectly capable of it.

'What is the point, Rohan? You will neglect me all over again for the four months I'll be there.'

'How dare you make me feel like this?' I explode. 'How dare you make me feel like I ill-treated you when all I did was sacrifice an entire life to be with you? We wouldn't even be married today if I hadn't moved to Delhi. Do you remember how *you* neglected *me* when I had just shifted? You wanted to be left alone to focus on your course. Day after day I hoped we would spend some time with each other and all you ever told me was you wanted to be left alone. But it's perfectly fine when you treat me like that. And if I do the same? Oh no! That is a *big* crime.'

Silence again. I can hear Ira cry softly. But I feel no remorse. I only want to cause her more pain.

'Ira?'

'Yes.'

'Is there another guy?'

There is deathly silence on the other end for a few seconds and then she bursts.

'I've been nothing but loyal to you, Rohan, all these years. And you have the *cheek* to ask me if there's another guy.'

Silence. She weeps. I know I shouldn't have said what I said but I can't apologize now. I am tired of being made to feel like everything is my fault.

'Are you unhappy, Ira?' I say.

'What—do—you—think? I have come this far just to be away from you and you're asking me if I'm unhappy.'

'No, listen to me. I know you are unhappy. Which is what I'm saying. Both of us hold so many things against each other and who's to say who's right? Maybe we are both right where we stand. And that means we are not right for each other. That's what I think.'

'Do you now?'

'Yes, I've been thinking about it for some time. About our relationship ...'

'I'm glad you are.'

'And I wonder if we are meant for each other.'

'Is that so?'

'If we can't make it work even after having known each other for ten years, maybe we've got something fundamental completely wrong.'

'Yes, it's a possibility. Certainly.'

'We've both made a lot of sacrifices ...'

'That we have.'

'... and in spite of those, it's not working ... the opposite has happened. We both hate each other almost.'

'Umm.'

'So I was thinking ...'

'Yes?'

'I know it will be difficult but it might be good for the both of us if ...'

'Yes?'

'If maybe we got a div—'

Ira hangs up. I stare at the Diagon Alley photo of her smiling on the brightly lit screen of my phone. After a minute, my face cracks and I start crying. I flip on the bed, crouch on my knees, my head bent into my chest, and I bawl. I half scream, half weep until Gaurav shakes me with force. I had forgotten he was in the room. I had forgotten I'm not home. Behind my closed eyes, my mind focused entirely on Ira, I had lost track of everything around me. There's someone knocking on the door, someone wondering what the commotion is about, but Gaurav ignores him. He only rubs my back, trying to calm me down—trying but failing.

10
Yusuf

I hit rock bottom over the next few weeks. There is massive, massive rage inside me which makes me do things I had thought I had outgrown with teenage. I deactivate my Facebook account and delete WhatsApp from my phone. I do not want to know or even be tempted to find out what's happening in Ira's life. She makes it easy by not trying to get in touch either. Somehow our separation in this virtual sphere feels more real than the one in the physical world.

I make no effort to hide the rage from the people around me. I tell Gaurav I do not want him coming over. Even by Delhi standards, I get needlessly aggressive with people ahead of me in queues in department stores. I meet Alisha over tea every day before work as per our routine but don't bother making small talk and stay silent throughout. She first realizes something is off when she tries to tell me she has taken up the ToI offer, and will be moving to Jaipur in a couple of months, and I have no reaction. I knew this was coming and had expected to feel bad about losing the daily company of someone I had grown to be fond of. I'm surprised that I'm not. I'm just glad that, on her last day in office, I'll be away in Kolkata for Tanuj's wedding.

She initially puts my grumpiness down to a bad day at work and lets me be. But, when the pattern continues, she tries to draw me out with pointed questions, to which I only grunt in response. She perhaps wonders if she is in some way responsible for my mood and I feel bad about doing this to her. One day she asks if we should stop meeting over tea. I say, 'No,' without attempting to explain my behaviour. But I try to be more congenial from then on.

Tanuj is less indulgent. After the first time I refuse when he asks me if I want to step out of office for a walk, he leaves me alone. I reason that he has wedding shopping, invitations and a thousand other things to worry about now. I am relieved that I don't have to justify myself, but I am also annoyed by how easily he gives up.

Typos never escape Maran's ever-observant hawk eyes, so the dramatic change in my approach to work has no chance. Once again he calls me into his room to ask what's going on, why the stories I am editing have questions waiting to be answered and language begging to be polished. I assure him I'll be more careful, but my heart isn't in it.

At least on workdays the only threat I pose is to news reports nobody will remember for more than a day. On the days I'm off, I am positively dangerous to Momo. I let his meal times pass and slap him when he nuzzles my hand. I feel bad immediately and put food in his bowl, but then he refuses to eat, whimpers and cowers under the bed when I go to stroke him. The sight of him breaks my heart and I tell myself that if I'm so ruthless to a helpless creature who is entirely dependent on me, there must be substance to Ira's allegations. From blaming her, I go to the other extreme and lose all faith in myself.

Sitting idle at home all day long, I select Ira's number on the phone to dial it but then think better of it. I decide to see a counsellor, only to realize they don't come cheap. All the ones I look up charge upwards of a grand per session. There's no way I can afford them. Then one day while editing a story about the rising number of suicides in the city, I chance upon a mention of the Sanjivini Society for Mental Health, which has a free counselling centre in Jangpura. I call and fix an appointment. But when the time comes, I get cold feet and freak out about talking about my problems with a total stranger, who, I imagine, will listen to my rant with detachment, all the while thinking, 'If I had a rupee for every time a man fought with his wife ...' I walk out of the reception without anyone knowing.

After giving up on the idea of seeking help, I decide to seek a lawyer. I imagine meeting Ira at the airport, getting her signature on the papers and both of us going our separate ways. But I find it harder to do this—to take this final, definitive step to end the past ten years of my life—than to make a fool of myself before a qualified doctor. So I wallow in self-pity day after day, refusing to buy vegetables, refusing to eat whatever Shobha throws together and refusing to get out of bed till I have to leave for office.

And then one afternoon, in the middle of getting ready for work, I drop on my bed and decide to lie there spreadeagled till some help arrives—and that's when the doorbell rings.

*

'Yusuf?'

'Surprise! Surprise!' the guy at the door chirps and engulfs me in a bear hug before I know what's going on. He holds me by the shoulders at arm's length and says, 'Oh thank god I caught you in time. They just *wouldn't* attach the aerobridge to the damn plane for half an hour after it landed and I kept thinking I'll have to sit on the stairs till you got back from work.' He then turns me around and walks me in.

'Who ... what—*what* are you doing here?' I jabber.

'Okay, brace yourself. I might just be moving back to Delhi! Have got an interview later today.'

'What? Really?' I say suspiciously.

'Hey! I expected a better reaction! You don't think I'm good enough to get a job offer or what?'

'No, no, of course not.' I'm still a little lost for words. 'Why didn't you tell me you were coming?'

'And miss the chance to see the look on your face? Where's the mirror? Come, you've got to see this.' He drags me to the mirror in the bathroom. 'You look so upset—like you're in bed with the hottest porn star ever but can't get things going!'

'Ha, ha, very funny.'

'No, seriously. You don't look too pumped about seeing me. Are you not pumped about seeing me, Rohan? Because that's a bother.'

'Of course I'm thrilled.'

'And what's with the beard and the red eyes?'

Out of nowhere, the lines from *The Catcher in the Rye* come to me, and I give Yusuf a long stare. He had once told me that they are his favourite lines in all of literature—that he likes to think of himself as the catcher in the rye. And I find myself reciting the lines in my head. It goes something like: 'I keep picturing all these little kids playing in this field of rye and all. And nobody's around—except me. What I have to do is catch everybody if they start to go over the cliff. That's all I'd do all day. I'd just be the catcher in the rye and all. I know it's crazy, but that's the only thing I'd really like to be.'

Aloud, I shrug and say, playing on these lines and what Yusuf had said as he held me by the shoulders after the bear hug at the door, 'You just caught me at a bad time. Thank god.'

*

The next day I throw an impromptu party in Yusuf's honour. It's the only day we have because he is to go back to Bangalore tomorrow. But since it's a Saturday, most of our common friends from journalism school are able to come for lunch. I also call Tanuj. He doesn't know anybody in the gathering other than me, but I want him to meet Yusuf.

Everybody loves Yusuf. Even though it's short notice, they come from far and wide to meet him. As usual, he is the life of the party. He regales them with stories—how he once started a petition for free Oreos in office, how he and his boss spend hours trolling each other on Facebook. Tanuj later tells me Yusuf exuded such warmth and took such genuine interest in their conversation that he ended up feeling he had known him for years. I had often wondered how Yusuf has this effect on people he meets for the first time. I guess that was it—he's genuine.

I take the day off, and in the evening we decide to go to Old Delhi for dinner. Although it's Saturday, there's considerable traffic on the way. As darkness falls, the traffic thickens, and we get stuck between two buses, an XUV and a Polo blaring Yo Yo Honey Singh near Pragati Maidan. After two days of respite, I once again start feeling blue thinking Yusuf will be gone soon.

'Tell me,' I say.

'Hmm?'

'You made up that job interview, right?'

'Wow, you figured. How?'

'I remember how much Mira used to hate Delhi. So I don't think you'd be considering a job here unless you guys are breaking up—which I don't think is the case.'

I'm looking at the road ahead but I can tell he is smiling at me. 'I always maintained you are the smartest man in the world, Rohan.' It's an old compliment and hardly sits well on me, but I am flattered.

It's start-stop traffic. We are stuck again before I can even move into second gear. 'So where did you go last evening—when I went to work?'

'To see an aunt who stays in Mayur Vihar. She isn't keeping too well. I wanted to meet her.'

'She was the reason you came to Delhi?'

'No, not really.'

'Then?'

'Gaurav called me last week to tell me you had a meltdown.' I did not see that coming and can feel my face go red. 'He didn't tell me what it was about. He asked me to speak to you. At first I thought you and Ira must have had one of your wild fights. But then I noticed you had gone off WhatsApp and Facebook too. That really got me worried.'

'Hah.' It's taken us twenty minutes just to get to the ITO junction. 'You call me smart and make me sound shallow at the same time.' Yusuf smiles.

There is silence for two minutes and I start to wonder why he isn't probing. 'You really spent all that money and came to Delhi because Gaurav told you I had a meltdown?'

'Didn't I tell you once that if we were fighting a war, like the First World War or the Second Peloponnesian War, and I had to leave you alone on the battlefield, I *would* come back for you eventually as the enemy advanced? Just staying true to my word.'

'Okay, I'm touched. But why haven't you asked me so far what's wrong?'

'Hey! I spent all that money and came to Delhi. I came back to the battlefield! Now it's up to you. I know you'll tell me. You are allowed as much time as you need.'

I don't say anything for two minutes. The traffic clears up after we have turned right and then taken a left on to the Ring Road. 'Ira and I did have one of our wild fights.'

'Okay,' he says. 'I don't think you need to worry too much. Haven't you guys been fighting for ten years? Didn't you go through a rough patch when you had just moved to Delhi? Didn't you guys break up once when you were dating? But you got back together, right? You always do. That's what makes you guys special. Together you're my favourite married couple!'

'But it's different this time.'

'How so?'

'Ira told me she went to New York *because* of me. Because she didn't want to be with me any more. You were my best man, Yusuf. You remember, on the day of the reception, Ira had gone to her place to dress up and come directly to the venue from there? I was restless the whole day and couldn't bear to be away from her. And finally when I saw her at the venue, I was so relieved. That feeling told me I was in love. And now look at us. We've gone seven months without seeing each other and it's like it doesn't affect us. Why aren't we going to pieces? I don't understand. For one whole month after we got married, I couldn't imagine being unhappy again. I was that overwhelmed with the joy of being married to the woman I loved. And now I can't remember the last time I felt happy. It's like it's only our legal commitment that's keeping us together, not any emotional one. What else do I make of her telling me she left because of me?'

'Look, I know you, and I know Ira too. I know you must have given her plenty of reasons to say so, but I also know that she is capable of saying these big things and taking drastic steps. But most of all I think it's the distance which is making her say these things. I'm sure once she is back for the summer and you spend some time with each other, you'll be fine. On your part, just make sure you are with her—in the moment ... It's so easy for most of us to be with people—you know, physically— but we aren't with them *in the moment*.'

He pauses, looks at me intently and continues, 'You remember T.S. Eliot's 'Waste Land'? There's a section where two lovers are talking, and one of them says, "Stay with me. Speak to me. Why do you never speak? What are you thinking of? I never know what you are thinking." To me, these are among the saddest lines ever written—this idea of two lovers sitting next to each other and feeling lonely.' My mind goes back to something Ira had once said. The road is clear now but I deliberately stay under fifty.

'Since we are talking literarily, I'll use Rowling,' I say. 'Horcruxes. In the books, horcruxes are bad. That's how Voldemort eludes death for years. But I don't think horcruxes are always bad. Or that it takes something as grave as murder to create one. We may not be consciously doing it, but we are splitting our souls all the time. There

111

is a part of my soul in Old Delhi, where we are going. It's where Ira and I had gone when I first came to Delhi to see her. There's a part of my soul in Sikkim, where I first experienced what it is to fall in love many years ago. Horcruxes, I think, are a way of life. They are a way of loving.'

I take a long pause. 'This marriage, and I know I sound silly when I put it like this,' I say, tearing up a little, 'is a horcrux. There's a huge part of my soul in it. But tell me, Yusuf, what happens when that part of the soul comes loose? What happens when the horcrux ceases to be one? Then it's simply an object without any worth, isn't it?'

This is the only way I can say it. It's the only way I can make sense of what I'm going through and expect Yusuf to get it. He doesn't respond. We have crossed Rajghat. The road is dark and empty and we are speeding towards our destination. I know there is a left turn here somewhere to get to the Red Fort parking lot, where I can leave the car and walk into Old Delhi.

'Yusuf?'

'Hmm?'

'For the first time I talked about divorce. And I meant it. That's what was scary. That's what made it more than one of our usual wild fights. It wasn't Ira throwing her temper. It was me talking about divorce. What do I do with this part of my soul that's come loose? What do I do with a dead horcrux? I don't know if our marriage will survive this year of distance. I don't know if we'll ever find all the lost love.'

I turn the mirror towards Yusuf as I enter the parking lot. 'Tell me, you've known both of us so long. Do you have any answers?'

There's a dim light from the street falling on him. Under it, I see a look of understanding pass over his face. And, without judgement, Yusuf, the ever wise one, only smiles. As if he has looked into the future and knows how my Second Peloponnesian War will end, but will not spoil the fun by telling me what he has seen. And, as always, I realize I'm taking myself less seriously than I was until a moment ago.

Love

Whatever I was looking for was always you.
Rumi

11
Arrival

It is May finally. For the last eight months it had loomed on the horizon, getting closer every day, yet seeming forever out of reach. So, now that it is here, it's a little difficult to believe.

Ira must be winding things up and packing her bags. But the fear hasn't left me that she might cancel her ticket if we fight one more time. So I've restricted our communication to the bare minimum. I avoid calling her. In my messages I keep the tone flat and business-like: what time is her flight, is she done packing, will she have to pay rent for the months she's gone. And she adopts the same tone in her texts to me. If she's sad about leaving New York and saying goodbyes to all her friends and Laura, she does not tell me. If she is dreading coming back and having to be in the same house with no one other than me, she does not tell me. It's like we have reached some sort of agreement on the code of conduct in the days before we meet again.

I have to be on my best behaviour—not only to ensure that she does in fact come back but also in the interest of a peaceful four months, which is the time I've decided to give our marriage. If things don't start looking up by the time she has to go back to New York in September, I will tell her again I want out. I've worked it out in my head.

It's not just the constant fights. We've had those before too. It's more to do with what they say in divorce cases: irreconcilable differences. It was a cliché until I experienced it first-hand. Now I do feel Ira and I have unbridgeable divides, interests that have been diverging little by little all these years—call it what you will. The more I've thought about it, the more I've accepted that I'm domestic. I want to have a steady job, build a career, be rooted in one place. Ira on the other hand wants to change cities and countries, not be tied down, and get a PhD perhaps. She is a wild spirit, an adventurous nomad—things I admire about her all right, but I don't see how we can make it work together. For a month I was sad that it should come to this. But I've had my day of reckoning.

And there is Tanuj's wedding, of course. It is to take place in Kolkata within a week of Ira's return. I do want to attend it, especially after he said I was the first person he invited and the only one who readily agreed to come despite the distance. I need peace to prevail so that Ira doesn't refuse to come along. Not showing up or, worse, showing up alone when Ira is back in Delhi are scenarios I'd like to avoid. She has told me in a text that she doesn't mind coming, but I have to ensure she is agreeable enough to oblige once she is here.

My mind wanders back to the laptop screen in front of me. It's night but the room is hot. The floor exudes heat, making me irritable. There is one last thing I have to do before I turn in. I had bought tickets for Ira and me on the Sealdah Express to Kolkata the day bookings opened. Now I go to the Air Vistara website and book us seats on a flight from Kolkata to Bagdogra two days after Tanuj's wedding, with a return to Delhi on the sixth of June, our second wedding anniversary.

*

Ira arrives in twelve hours, which seems like enough time to do all the things I have planned. I scrub the bathroom floor, shine the taps, clean the kitchen platform with soap water, lay fresh sheets of newspaper in the drawers and neatly stack the utensils on them, remove cobwebs from the nooks between the ceiling and the walls and dust the photo frames. Just getting the slimy, thick layer of oil off the blades of the exhaust fan in the kitchen takes up an hour. By the end of it, my fingers are blistered and burning. When I look up at the wall clock, I'm stunned to see it's three-thirty. I'm an hour behind.

I get into a T-shirt and jeans, pick up my car keys and rush to INA Market to buy fresh fish and coconut milk. I had learnt to cook from Ira but I never learnt to enjoy it. It remained a cause of discord between us even after we got married. She would get angry with me for refusing to help out in the kitchen and would say that cooking together is something that would bring us closer. I would scoff and refuse to give in.

But today is her day. The first thing she should taste after being away for eight months should be her favourite prawn curry with rice and fried pomfret.

It's almost five by the time I get back, and I start sprinting from one thing to the next. I put the prawns in a bowl of hot water to defrost them. I get my laptop and look up the recipe online. I chop onions, chillies and tomatoes and arrange all the spices I need in a line. Then I take a saucepan and heat a tablespoon of oil in it, adding mustard seeds, chopped onions, a bit of turmeric powder, some whole pepper and cardamom. But when I add dried red chillies, the mixture immediately turns black and there's a blast of smoke that makes me cough. I turn off the gas, realizing that I added the chillies too late and I will have to start from scratch. One look at the clock and I'm almost in tears. I don't want to mess things up on the day Ira is returning. For a moment I toy with the idea of taking her to an expensive restaurant for dinner straight from the airport. But I set the thought aside with a mental note that that is an escape route I've always taken and tonight needs to be different.

Feeling thoroughly overwhelmed, I set about chopping the onions all over again. Thankfully, this time around, I remember what Ira had once said: 'There are only two differences between the food Shobha cooks and what I make—love and low flame.' So, instead of rushing things, I slow down. I pass the first test by not creating a black, soggy mess a second time. After pouring a mug of water into the saucepan and adding the prawns, tomato puree and coconut milk, I put a lid on it to let the curry simmer and come to a boil. When I take off the lid ten minutes later, I'm greeted with a delicious aroma that immediately makes my stomach growl and I know even before I've tasted the curry that I've got it right.

Next, I measure a cup of rice, wash it thoroughly, immerse it in water in a container and put it on the stove. On the chopping board I create a mix of turmeric and red chilli powders, salt and water. In a second saucepan I heat two tablespoons of oil. I coat the slices of pomfret with the mix and drop them in. The kitchen is full of the smell of fish. The pomfret takes a long time to turn the perfect shade of crispy golden brown but I'm patient. One by one I fry the fish as the clock ticks, hoping that the taste, despite my lack of practice, will carry me through.

After I've finished cooking, I stare at the clock and the sink. Great food sitting alongside unwashed vessels will do me no good, and so I start doing the dishes in spite of knowing that I'm cutting it too close.

Momo is restless all through my four hours in the kitchen. At first I think it's the smell of the fish that's driving him crazy and I give him some food. But he keeps running about the house, rolling on the floor and imploring me to open the kitchen door. When I do, he runs to the bedroom and slips under the bed. I look under and assure him I'm not going to hit him. He comes out and starts to bark wildly, thwacking me with his fat paws. I don't know what is wrong with him. Perhaps there's going to be an earthquake. Just to get him out of the way,

I put him in his cage and dart into the bathroom for a nice long shower. As I look at my bathrobe hanging from a hook on the back of the door, I note in passing that, come tomorrow, there will be Ira's next to it once more, and I feel oddly happy. The pleasantly tepid summer water relaxes me and I lose track of time. I regret it when I come out of the bathroom and realize that Ira's flight lands in fifteen minutes. Even if immigration keeps her for half an hour, I barely have enough time to reach the airport, park my car and stand at the arrival gate in time for the first glimpse of her emerging from the terminal.

I quickly wear my jeans and a black full-sleeve shirt with dark blue stripes that Ira had once long back told me I look handsome in. I turn out the lights and am about to close the main door behind me when Momo gives out a pitiful yowl from inside his cage. I don't want an angry Anju to be the first thing greeting Ira on reaching home, so I go back in, put Momo on his leash and put him in the back seat of the car. 'Idiot,' I say to him sternly. 'If you dribble on my seat, I'll leave you at the airport.' He looks terrified and I laugh.

Thankfully, there's no traffic and I weave in and out of gaps between exasperatingly slow-moving cars and reach T3 at five minutes past eleven. Her flight was scheduled to land at ten-fifty. I am running late. The underground parking lot echoes with a shrill screech as I drive into the first empty spot I see and jump on the brake. I leave Momo looking bewildered behind the window pane and lock the doors with the remote.

T3 is a huge terminal and has several levels. I lose a minute just waiting for the lift to come down to the basement. Once I'm out two floors above, I break into a run like my life depends on it—down corridors, up escalators and finally along the waiting area outside the arrival gates. I stop for breath and look up at a flight information display screen. Ira's Jet Airways flight via Brussels has landed. If it did as per schedule, I say to myself as I look at my watch, she would be out of the terminal by now. I start looking through the crowd for her familiar face. There are cars speeding and stopping, men and women hugging and letting go, people crossing each other's paths with trolleys. I didn't want to call Ira because I thought spotting her in the crowd would be fun, but now I am afraid I may have missed her.

That is when I see her in the distance. She is at least a hundred feet away, turning a corner and emerging out of an arrival gate. She only has a backpack sitting heavily on her shoulders. She looks around but doesn't see me. Once, a few weeks back, during a short spell when we weren't fighting, she had told me that she had cut her hair. I've known her thirteen years but it's the first time I see her with hair that ends at her neck. She looks ... different. But other than the hair, she's in the same full-sleeve blue-and-red check shirt and beige corduroys that she had worn on the day of her departure. In her hand she holds a large KFC Krushers plastic cup covered with a dome-shaped lid, drinking out of it through a straw. She sees me now as we draw closer.

I had gone over this moment in my head several times and wondered how it would play out. But I am not prepared for how it does. We don't run towards each other like characters in films. We don't even smile. As we come within a foot of each other, her lips still closed around the straw, she looks up at me tentatively, a little vulnerably, as if to ask if I will treat her well this time. She makes me aware of my power over her, not physical but emotional, and I embrace her tightly.

There's no overwhelming burst of emotions. I take the backpack from her shoulders and we start walking to the parking lot. A little formally, I ask her how her flight was, if she managed to get enough sleep, if she's jetlagged. She answers the questions and we are civil on the whole. As we step out of the lift, I start walking ahead of her because I want to get out of the parking lot before the first half hour is over. I dump her backpack inside and leave the door open for Momo to see Ira.

He looks from me to her. At first his face seems blank, or at least impassive. But as she smiles and screams his name—I hadn't told her Momo is in the car—he barks loudly, jumps out and, without allowing me time or even a reflex to catch his flying leash, goes bounding towards Ira. He leaps at her with such force that she is knocked off her feet, and he starts slobbering all over her face as she falls down to her knees without protest.

If I can see her face through his fur, I think she is a little teary-eyed. Dare I say she is home?

12
Wedding

Ira and I are like new acquaintances in the car. The awkwardness, the wait for the destination to arrive, the hunt for things to say—a third person could hardly tell we have known each other for years. But, at the same time, there's no mention of the last time we spoke, and I'm glad to avoid that conversation. I wonder if the silence is temporary before the inevitable talk finally takes place or if Ira too has decided to take the next four months as they come. I choose not to ask.

As I turn on the lights in the flat and enter, she walks from room to room to familiarize herself again to the place we called home. She criticizes my rearrangements of the furniture and says that I have no taste as she one by one notices the new things I've acquired over the past year. But she says this without the sting of our fights, and through it all I'm oddly pleased that she retains her sense of ownership towards our rented home despite setting up a new life for herself elsewhere.

What really bugs me is that she fails to notice, even after seeing me change in the full glare of the tube light, that I have finally lost the paunch she was after me for years to lose. So when she asks me, 'What's for dinner?' I look guilty and tell her I thought she would have eaten on the plane. Her face falls and I quickly suggest going out for a bite to Potbelly. It's only when she starts to look really upset that I lead her to the kitchen, take the lids off the pans and direct the aroma of the prawns and the pomfret towards her nose. Perhaps to punish me she does not praise the food when we sit down to eat. She tells me not to expect her to be grateful that I have cooked for her for the first time since we got married. But when I wake up startled at four that morning to see her helping herself to a second dinner in bed according to New York time, it feels like recognition enough for all the hard work. Gratified, I put an arm around her waist, for the first time in eight months, and go back to sleep.

*

My attempt to keep Anju away from Ira is not so successful. The next morning I'm reading the newspaper on the pot when the doorbell rings. At first, I assume it's Shobha, but then I hear loud voices from the door. I can tell it's Anju but fail to imagine what it could be this time. Momo has been calm after Ira returned and threw open all the doors that I would keep shut to prevent him from chewing up footwear and cushions and pillows. I rush out and appear at the door behind Ira as Anju stands outside and screams. Neighbours watch from behind their safety doors.

'See, just see what a ruckus he makes,' she says. I have to push Momo away to stop him barking at Anju.

'Dogs do that,' Ira says, trying to sound reasonable. 'For him, you're just a stranger at the door. I'm sure he doesn't make noise like this otherwise.'

'What do you know?' she snaps back. 'You haven't been here for months. Ask your husband if you don't believe me. He has faced the worst of it.'

I see what she is trying to do. 'What happened now?' I ask, not letting the landlady enlist me on her side.

'The dog pooped outside my door,' Anju declares dramatically.

'He has been home all morning,' I say.

'How do I know that? How do I know he didn't do it last night when I saw you two take him upstairs? I'm no expert at analysing how fresh poop is.'

'Listen,' Ira says, and I can tell she is getting angry—not because of the allegation but because Anju won't stop shouting. 'Our dog is trained. Maybe it is some other dog who did it.'

'Twenty years we have lived here and no dog has ever dared to shit outside our house,' she says, even louder this time. 'Even if it's some other dog, he's coming upstairs only to meet yours, I'm sure. They know there's another of their species living here, thanks to all the noise he makes. It's his fault if they are treating this building as their toilet now.'

And before Ira can say a word, I match Anju's tone and shout back, taking even myself by surprise, 'We can't help what a stray dog does outside your house. Please don't create a scene outside ours and ruin our morning. If you have a problem with us, give us one month's notice and we'll vacate the place.'

Anju looks too stunned to say anything. I know Sunil well and he is not the sort to care more about a mutt than his money. There aren't too many tenants willing to pay twenty thousand in Shahpur Jat.

'You're being very uncooperative,' she says. 'You won't even come downstairs and take a look.'

'What for?'

'You know, I didn't even say bye to my children when they left for school. I was *that* disturbed after I opened the door and stepped into the poop. What a way to begin my day! And you can't even come and see what has happened.'

I want to tell Anju that her children are teenagers and do not care that she did not see them off to school. But I restrain myself and say, 'Look, we have already told you it's not our dog who has done this. You better find out who has and deal with him.'

I make to shut the door but Anju is not done. She turns to Ira and says, 'You are the one who got him, aren't you? I had seen you carry him home that day. You shouldn't have got him if you didn't want to look after him. It's the first rule of being parents also. Check your capability before you add to your responsibility.'

'*Our* responsibility,' I snarl back. 'Momo is not her responsibility but ours. And one of us is perfectly capable of looking after him. Thank you.'

I slam the door in Anju's face and, breathing heavily, sit on the sofa, trying to resume reading the newspaper. Ira sits next to me. I wonder if she will scold me for losing my cool or for offering to move out. She is here only for four months and I'm sure does not want to spend those house hunting all over again. But she takes my hand in hers and says softly, 'We'll figure out what to do. Don't be upset, okay?'

'Yes, all right,' I shrug and say. 'But what if Anju comes complaining and picks up a fight with Gaurav while we are gone?'

'I'm sure he'll be fine. It's not the first time he'll be here looking after Momo in our absence.'

I'm not convinced, but there's nothing we can do till we are back. 'Let's start packing,' I say. 'We're going to be gone for two weeks.'

*

The lanes of Behala resonate with the sound of ululations, which tells us we are nearing Tanvi's home. Ira and I are in the back seat of an old Maruti 800 in which Tanvi's brother-in-law picked us up from Sealdah station, feeling alien in a land whose language we don't understand. We look out, taking in the sight of the big, discolouring houses and of the people going about their day languidly on bicycles, seeming simpler and friendlier than the ones we are used to in Delhi.

The wedding is to take place in this small suburb of Kolkata where Tanvi's parents live. Tanuj and his family from Bombay have gathered at his aunt's house not far from here. They are to come to the hall only around lunch, but he wanted us to meet Tanvi first. I expect to feel out of place until he arrives. We get out of the car and push open the gate of a two-storied house where everybody knows everybody else but us. The narrow staircase rings with the sound of laughter and round Bengali syllables. I quickly reach out for Ira's hand and enclose mine in it.

'Come, come,' says a tall and lean elderly man with a beard in a soft voice as we step in side by side. 'You must be Tanuj's friends. I hope you had a good journey.' I presume he is Tanvi's father. Ira and I nod and sit down on the sofa as the others squeeze closer together for us. 'May is not the best time to get married in Kolkata,' he continues, offering us water. 'It gets very hot and humid. People sweat a lot and build up an appetite for all the fish, though!' he laughs, adding, 'But Tanu's wedding is at night, as most Bengali weddings are. So it won't be very uncomfortable.'

I nod politely as he gets a call from the caterer and excuses himself. Another relative comes out of the kitchen and offers us tea. The house is full of twenty to thirty men and women milling about in finery, while Ira and I sit in sweat-soaked clothes from yesterday. I look around to see if I can spot Tanvi.

'Hi,' says a woman who emerges from a bedroom, cradling a baby in her left arm. From a photo Tanuj had shown me of the two families, taken on the terrace of his house the day the wedding was fixed, I can tell this is Tanvi's elder sister. 'Tanvi will be out in a minute,' she says as she sits in the chair vacated by her father. She looks a bit frazzled.

'And who might this be?' Ira asks the baby, putting out her hand. 'Shake hands?'

'She's Polka. That's the only word she answers to anyway.'

Polka not only shakes the hand but unexpectedly and eagerly goes from her mother's arm to Ira's. 'Tanuj and I worked together once, but I'm sure you know him better,' Tanvi's sister says. 'And since you are here and he is not, how about you tell us all we need to know about him?'

I laugh, relax and say, 'He warned me I would be probed and told me strictly not to answer any trick questions. I will not give him away.'

She laughs too and, leaving Polka to honk Ira's nose, goes back in to check what's keeping Tanvi. I get my phone out to take photos of the two. Polka, we discover, loves being photographed. She strikes one pose after another for the camera as her audience laughs and applauds. I am busy focusing from her to Ira when Tanvi comes out, looking beautiful in a yellow Bengali cotton sari and red blouse that covers her back and arms. She is younger than Ira and me but, with her hair tied in a bun, looks lady-like and older than her years. Her eyes narrow as she looks at us and smiles. Tanuj had told me she herself does not like this narrowing of her eyes when she smiles as she feels it makes her look foreign. But I find it endearing.

131

'Hi Rohan. Hi Ira,' she says warmly. Her voice is sweet and clear and evidently trained in music. 'It's so good to meet you guys finally. Tanuj has told me so much about you.'

And as she sits down to talk, I quickly send him a message, partly as reassurance and partly because I feel it's the right thing to say: 'Good choice.'

*

Ira and I have been put up in one of the rooms at the wedding venue, which is also where arrangements have been made for lunch for the two families and us. So we head there after meeting Tanvi. Tanuj and his family arrive at noon. There's something unmissable about him that says he is the star of the whole affair. It's not what he's wearing; the wedding does not start for another twelve hours and he is in a plain yellow collared T-shirt and jeans that he would wear on an average day in Delhi. It's more to do with the way he carries himself. He does not look stressed or apprehensive but revels in the attention he receives from his family and Tanvi's. He does not eat with the rest of the party but goes from table to table to ask after the guests. He is a man in control.

As always I overeat, particularly the fish, and slip into a food coma as soon as Ira and I retire to our room. It's evening by the time she wakes me up. I look out of the window of our room and see that preparations in the lawn are already in top gear. I rush to the bathroom and have a quick bath before changing into the maroon sherwani I've got. While Ira gets ready, I decide to go downstairs and look around.

Strings of fairy lights dropped from the terrace come to life just as I walk on to the lawn. Guests begin to arrive and a crowd gathers around the food counter. Tanvi sits nervously in a throne in one hall adjacent to the lawn as her friends keep her company. As per the custom, the groom is detained in a different hall until the start of the ceremony a few hours later. He is in a cream-coloured silk dhoti and a richly embroidered dark red kurta. The cone-shaped topor he wears on his head signals that he is ready for the marriage. His shoot is over. As I enter, he is explaining to the photographer that once the ceremony is done, he wants him to take a photo that would resemble the poster of *Tanu Weds Manu*—the groom seated in his wedding clothes with Tanvi next to him in hers, her legs stretched over the arms of the throne after she has passed out against his shoulder. Tanuj tells him he will put it up on Facebook with the caption 'Tanu Weds Tanu'.

'Best man,' he says as I go up and sit beside him.

'Am I?'

'Of course.'

'So, as best man, what can I do you for? Are you thinking of running away? Do I need to counsel you?'

'What? No! I'm happy and I'm excited. I can't wait to be married.'

I cock an eyebrow at him. 'Really?' I say. 'I knew Ira for ten years when we got married, and *I* wasn't so excited. You can be honest with me.'

'I am,' he asserts. 'True story. I know my life is about to change but I'm not scared. I feel prepared.'

I scoff disbelievingly. 'Okay seriously,' I say. 'You never told me the whole story.'

'Didn't I? I told you it was serendipity. That's all there was to it, really.' He stares at me stare at him and adds, 'Okay, I'll tell you one more thing from that day I met her for the first time. I lay all my cards on the table. I told her how much money I make and what sort of life I'm capable of giving her. She later told me she liked that about me—that I was honest. That's what made her choose me. You know, Rohan, you and I—we have a lot to be grateful for. We ought to be grateful that the girls who chose to marry us did so in spite of a lot of odds. Which is why I'm looking forward to what lies ahead. It can only be fun, right?'

I look at him without answer. 'How's Ira?' he asks.

'All right.'

'You know, if you want me to assign you one best-man duty, it would be to be with her. I wouldn't want her to feel out of place. There are enough people to fuss over me; you should go be with her.'

*

I find that Ira is ready when I go back upstairs. She only asks me to hook the mangalsutra, which she wears on traditional occasions, behind her neck. She has a scent of rosewater and looks like a dream. I had wanted her to wear the green Kanjivaram silk sari from my brother's wedding two years ago. But she reminded me it's going to be hot and humid here and so chose a maroon cotton sari instead to go with my sherwani. Though it wasn't my first choice, I concede that it's better for the night ceremony than the green would have been.

We go downstairs and are greeted jovially at every step by members of Tanuj's family who keep us occupied and entertained. We are licking our fingers at the end of dinner after several helpings of the bhetki paturi when we see Tanvi being carried on a wooden seat by her brothers and uncles, the shy smile on her face hidden behind the two betel leaves she holds in her hands. We quickly finish eating and hurry on to the mandap. Most guests have dined and left by now and only close family members gather around; that is the way of a traditional Bengali wedding, we are told. It is midnight.

The main wedding ritual begins with Tanvi encircling Tanuj seven times. As the pandits keep up their chant of mantras, the bride and groom stand facing each other. She lowers the betel leaves and their eyes finally meet. Tanuj covers the parting of Tanvi's hair with sindoor. Ululation ensues. Conch shells go off. They are now officially married. But the rituals are not yet over. They go on for another hour as the onlookers start petering out and there are only a handful left. Throughout, Tanuj has about him what he likes to call the look of optimism. It is the expression he summons to his face every time he poses for a photo or knows he is being watched. It is not really an expression of happiness. He does not exactly smile. But with the subtlest adjustment of the muscles of his eyes and mouth, he conveys to his audience that good things are about to happen to him.

Ira sits by herself on a step at the edge of the mandap as I walk around to take photos on my phone. I take one of her from a distance: her chin rests on her palm as she watches the proceedings, looking impassive and thoughtful, unbothered by the late hour and the heat. I feel a surge of gratitude for her for having come with me without a fuss within days of returning from New York, simply because it was something I wanted to do. I feel thankful that she hasn't brought up our recent fights so far and yet again wonder if she will some time soon. Her face is inscrutable. I don't know what she's thinking. Is she working on an argument? Or has she put all of it behind? Will our marriage survive the differences that have surfaced? We may not be fighting right now but I know our relationship is not what it used to be. I don't know how to fix it—or even what it is that needs fixing.

As I look from Ira to Tanvi and Tanuj, I wonder if our marriage would have been less complicated if we belonged to the same communities and had got married as per tradition, not in court. It's a silly thought, I know, but I entertain it only because I'm at a loss for answers and I'm looking for them in places where I wouldn't have looked before. Would Ira and I be happier if we had decided to live in like Yusuf and Mira instead of getting married? Would it have been better for me if I had an arranged marriage? I think of Alisha getting on a train to Jaipur in a few hours from now. Would I be happier had

I stayed single like her? What would it be like to start a life with someone new without the baggage of a decade?

As the rituals conclude and Tanuj and Tanvi proceed to feast with their families, Ira and I head back to our room. We change into our bedclothes and Ira falls asleep before the lights are out. Even in sleep, she looks tired but uncomplaining. I stay up a few minutes longer, thinking of the ten days that lie ahead. Ira and I will finally be without a buffer between us. And left to our own devices, there's no knowing what we might do.

13
Holiday

Sikkim is special to me—has been for many years now. It is where I first experienced what falling in love is. I think a love for your parents is something you are born with. And the friends you make at a young age, more than anything else, are accidental companions you grow used to over time. So when you first *fall* in love, it's a feeling you've never imagined before. It takes your breath away, it moves the ground beneath your feet. But, most of all, it moves something inside you. For me, Sikkim was where it happened.

It was at the end of my first year of college. An ex-student who had started a travel company had organized a trip to Sikkim as part of the adventure club in college and I had immediately signed up. I did not know anyone else who was going, but I was instinctively drawn to the place. After a day's journey from Bombay to Kolkata, followed by an overnight train to New Jalpaiguri, we had finally driven in a packed, noisy bus into the mist of the mountains.

At the end of the long journey, though, I found Sikkim a bit underwhelming. It had sounded remote and exotic but what I saw was unexceptional. Honestly, it seemed like any other place in the Himalayas I had been to before. Worse, I was told our hotel would have a beautiful view of the valley. But, as things turned out, I could barely see my own nose—the fog was that thick.

The next morning, I was startled out of sleep by a general commotion in the corridor outside. Frightened and disoriented, I saw it was barely seven o'clock. My roommate, a junior I had befriended on the train, wasn't around. I threw my blanket away, hurriedly put on my sweatshirt and stepped out on to the corridor facing the valley. And there it was, right in front of me. Hidden the previous day, it now seemed so close that I could make out its contours, its shadows and almost the texture of its snow. I ate my words and conceded it was unlike anything I had seen before. Mount Kanchenjunga, the third highest mountain in the world, its heights swathed in the pearly pink light of daybreak, looked old yet ageless, tall and stoic. Ironically, it was something so still and unmoving that moved something inside me, and right there, unable to take my eyes off it for several minutes, I fell in love for the very first time.

So when the time came for me to plan an anniversary holiday for Ira and me, the first place I thought of was Sikkim. It's been ten years but the memory of that morning is still fresh. And I hoped, in my own uncertain agnostic way, that the place where I first fell in love might also lead me to rediscover what I have lost.

*

But I begin to regret my impulsive and irrational choice long before we are anywhere near Sikkim. It is a clear, sunny day in Kolkata when we take off, so Ira decides not to take an Avomine and instead stay awake for our first time on a Vistara flight. As with most things, my airline selection was guided by the criterion of cost. But now that we are on the plane, we realize we have actually got a good deal. We are about to pass up the airhostess's meal offer when we find out that we don't have to pay separately for it, and, even better, it's not just salad and rice with one piece of chicken but a full plate of prawn lasagne, with chocolate fondant for dessert. We relish the wholesome meal supplied by Taj and take out our copy of the *Lonely Planet Sikkim* guide, knowing well that we will soon succumb to sleep. And that is when it happens. The plane jumps several feet in the air as people gasp and look at each other in fright.

Ira immediately reaches for the air sickness bag in the seat pocket and throws up. A short, soft beep rings down the aisle, the overhead seatbelt indicator lights up and the captain's voice comes on the intercom, informing us that we are passing through a particularly bad stretch of turbulence and asking us to return to our seats. I see fat droplets of water slide down the other side of the window panes. There's a downpour outside.

I call the airhostess and hand her Ira's air sickness bag, hoping that this is the one bad thing that has to happen at the start of a good holiday. I wait for the rain to stop as suddenly as it had started, for the sun to emerge and for the scary and sickening shuddering of the aircraft to come to an end. Since none of it happens, I ask Ira if she wants to take an Avomine. But we are only minutes from landing and popping the tablet now would mean she will be drowsy for the rest of the day, so she refuses. I feel bad for her. I take her hand in mine as she rests her head against my shoulder, swallowing hard to fight the nausea.

Instead of easing up, the turbulence only becomes worse. I too start to feel like I want to throw up as the plane starts descending. This has never happened to me before, so I dig my nails into the arms of my seat and stare at the roof, trying not to be affected by the panic that has set in around me. A sideways glance at Ira tells me she is about to vomit again. I get the air sickness bag out of my seat pocket and hold it open before her mouth just as she retches hard.

The massive wave of relief that washes over me as the plane touches down in Bagdogra recedes too quickly. The only prepaid taxi counter at the airport is crowded with tourists and locals trying to get to Siliguri and Darjeeling, and cabs are in short supply. I have to stand at the window for twenty minutes, jostling with the unruly lot of people as my whole body breaks into a sweat in the high humidity, before I can get a booking for five hundred rupees for a short ride to Siliguri. Outside in the porch, Ira stands by weakly while I look up at the heavy downpour, waiting for our driver to arrive.

He is a jolly fellow who tells us as he looks at us in the mirror five minutes into the drive that monsoon has arrived in Bengal ahead of schedule this year. I ask him hopefully if it's raining less heavily in the hills. To which he inconsiderately says no. Ira and I look at each other and smile at the same moment in spite of ourselves.

It is evening by the time we arrive at the Siliguri hotel where we are to spend the night. Despite the hunger, all I want to do when I drop in the bed is sleep off. But the next day's arrangements are yet to be made. Gaurav's travel agent friend, Sharmila, through whom I have made most of the bookings for the holiday, had told me she could arrange a taxi to drive us from Siliguri to Gangtok. But it would have cost us a good sum and we are on a shoestring budget, so I had turned her down.

I must now step out in the rain and the diminishing light to book bus tickets for tomorrow. Thankfully, our hotel is in the main market and I am told I can walk down to the Sikkim National Transport bus stand, but when I get there I find it deserted. An enthusiastic guard tells me with a resourceful air that buses have stopped plying from the SNT stand to Gangtok and directs me instead to the Tenzing Norgay bus terminus a few metres away on the other side of the road. This one is full of activity and chaos, but a passing conductor tells me I can buy tickets only once I'm on the bus tomorrow. This means running the risk of passing up one packed bus after another before we can manage to get seats, and that could take hours as there is a service to Gangtok only once every half hour. The buses themselves look so rickety and battered that I can tell the journey will be very uncomfortable. In deep despair I decide to call up Sharmila and ask her to send us a taxi.

That is when the first good thing of the day happens. Sharmila tells me there is a third option. A shared taxi. She says it is the locals' most favoured mode of transport to get to Gangtok and guides me over the phone to the place in the market from where we can get a shared taxi the next morning.

I sleep uneasily despite the exhaustion and we set out early soon after breakfast. The taxis are old Boleros that seat ten people plus the driver: two in front, four in the middle and four at the back. The first six seats, which are likely to be the least shaky and jumpy in the uphill drive on bad roads, are all taken, but Ira is not willing to wait for another taxi. Finding enough passengers before it departs would mean we would have to hang around for at least an hour, and she is eager to reach Gangtok and get some proper rest. So we accept the seats in the back, booking all four to ensure comfort, and our taxi sets off.

The drive is quiet and uneventful and lasts all morning. Ira sleeps through most of it, her head resting on my shoulder as I idly fiddle with my phone. As we stop and step out for lunch at a small wayside restaurant that also doubles up as the owner's house, I breathe deeply in the hope that we have left the bad part of our holiday behind along with the plains. The dense green of the mountains is encouraging and I feel like I can be upbeat.

But this new optimism lasts only a few hours. As has happened since our flight took off from Kolkata, I am let down soon enough. When we enter Gangtok I realize that the town is more touristy and less undiscovered than I remember it to have been ten years ago, a drizzle if not a downpour has followed us here, and the mountain air isn't refreshing. It is heavy with diesel fumes from all the ancient shared taxis converging from the plains and the different parts of Sikkim into the capital of the state. Our hotel room overlooks a valley all right, but the view is broken by the roofs of several hotels further down the slope, and there is nothing remotely as spectacular as the Kanchenjunga on the horizon. As Ira steps into the bathroom to freshen up, I remain standing in the sunless late-afternoon light on the balcony, feeling miserable that my estimations of the weather, the cost and, most importantly, the destination have all gone wrong.

*

Ira and I have nice, relaxing hot-water baths and sleep cosily through the afternoon under the rajai. With the lights out and curtains drawn, I'm a bit disoriented when I wake up to find myself in darkness several hours later. I am uncertain if it is late night or early morning, but when I check my phone, I see it is only six-thirty in the evening. I have a childhood tendency to feel blue if I wake up at dusk from deep sleep, and it happens to me now. Something feels off, so I go out on the balcony without waking Ira and dial Amma's number.

She sounds pleased to get a call from me. She enquires about the journey, the cold and, after asking in detail what I had for breakfast and lunch, tells me to be careful about what I eat while travelling. She reminds me that I am prone to falling sick with the slightest change of weather and asks if I am wearing enough warm clothes. I answer all her questions tediously, mostly in affirmative or negative grunts. She then passes the phone to Appa. I talk to him about this and that for a few minutes and then hang up. But it's reassuring just to hear their voices. They belong to a time when nothing felt out of place.

Pinpricks of lights come alive in the valley. As I can't make out much else in the dark, I stretch an arm beyond the balcony railing to see if it's still raining. It's not. I go back in and see that Ira is awake. Turning on the lights, I realize it will be too depressing to order dinner to the room, so I suggest going to the main market in the town centre instead. Ira splashes her face with water and puts kohl in her eyes. We wear our thermals and sweaters and step out, our hands dug deep into our pockets. We ask the girl at the reception to call us a cab but she says it will cost us two hundred rupees for the short distance of two kilometres. It is like this in touristy hill stations, she says sagely, and we decide to walk.

There is an awkward silence between Ira and me for two minutes as we start on the dark road that slopes up and down in the distance. Then in my infinite wisdom I dive head-first into the conversation I have been trying to avoid ever since Ira returned.

'Do you want to talk about the D word?' I blurt out.

'The D word?'

'Divorce.'

Ira doesn't stop walking but looks round at me and merely smiles in her usual pithy way that makes me feel stupid. 'Do you?' she asks.

'Not really. But I feel like there is something hanging between us. So maybe we should talk about it.'

'Okay, let's.'

After the abrupt start, I'm lost for words. 'Are you having a good time?' I ask tentatively.

'I'm all right,' she says. And before I know it, she veers off in a different direction with, 'But what *were* you thinking getting us here!'

I want to cry. 'You don't like the place?' I ask.

'It's not that I don't like it. But we are in the hills right at the start of monsoon.'

'Monsoon's arrived early this year,' I whine, parroting our Bagdogra driver. 'Not my fault.'

'It's still June and the rains are unpredictable in the north-east. You should've read up a bit, no?'

'But it's monsoon all over India at this time. *You* should have listened to me when I was saying we should get married in December—such wonderful weather everywhere.'

The smile again.

'You know,' I say, 'sometimes I think you insisted on June just because the only place with good weather at this time for anniversary vacations would be Europe.'

Ira laughs and I feel at ease. 'Of course, that was the reason,' she says.

146

'Listen, I can't afford Europe, okay? I can barely afford Sikkim.'

'How much are we blowing on it, by the way?'

'I had estimated forty, but now I think fifty, which means we'll end up spending something like sixty.'

'You could've bought a return ticket to New York in that much, I hope you know that.'

'Yes, I do.'

'You should legally never be permitted to handle money,' she says. 'Just send it all to me.'

'Don't rub it in now.'

'Rub in what?'

'The whole money thing. You know, sometimes I think we've been fighting so much because ... we wouldn't have fought so much if I made more money. There's a reason why Tanuj can marry a stranger and know he can make her happy. There's a reason why my brother has and my parents have had the perfect marriage. Money. I've been thinking about it and I've decided I'm going to switch to corp comm or something.'

'Sure. Because that's what you want to do in life.'

'No, it isn't but ...'

'Rohan, why are you always like this? Why are you always looking for answers in the wrong things?' I now regret having started this conversation. We may not have been having a good time earlier, but things are positively heating up now. The dark road is also winding endlessly and only making us pant; the market is nowhere in sight.

'What do you ...?'

'Rohan, have I ever complained to you about money? Have I ever asked you to make more money? It's all in your head. You used to complain when I used to give you all my income. And you complain now because of the cutbacks we have to make because of the small loan you had to take. There are days in New York when I just have a block of cheese for dinner, but I don't badger you to send me more money. I know I'm doing the best I can and so are you.'

'So you wouldn't have minded if I hadn't taken you on an expensive anniversary holiday?'

'I would have liked to go away with you anyplace we can afford. I *did not* want you spending a bomb on coming all the way to Sikkim when it's raining.'

'And you don't want me to do a job that'll pay more?'

'Of course not if that's not what you want to ... I don't know where you've got this idea that you need to be this *man*—this provider of the family. You're supporting me today and some day I will support you. We were never going to be this traditional couple with traditional gender roles ... This is what I don't like about you, Rohan.'

'What?' I sound timid even to myself.

'You blow up these things in your mind that I've never said a word about because you find it easier to wrap your head around them. While the things that I do discuss with you—the things that actually matter to me—you never seem to get around to those.'

'What are you talking about?'

'We *haven't* been fighting because you don't make enough money. We've been fighting—I went away to New

York—because I didn't feel you cared for what is good for me. You promised me a life of happiness, Rohan. I wanted to marry you because I felt you will always look out for me and with you I will be able to grow. I always think about what's good for you, don't I? I tell you not to move to corp comm even if it gets you more money because I know it won't be good for you. But you didn't do that for me. That entire time I was upset about my job, not once did you say—Quit if you are that unhappy. Not once did you ask yourself if it was good for me—if it would make me happy. That is why I thought about it and took the decision myself without taking you into account. Even after I got accepted for my course, did you help me with the paperwork? Did you help me pack? You took a loan for me and let me go, so you thought you had done your bit. But I know deep down you were angry at me for going. You may not admit it to yourself, but you resented me for leaving you behind alone. And all the anger and resentment came to the surface the first time we had a fight. You felt entitled to ask me to keep my work aside and make time for you because, in your head, you were the good, understanding husband who had been wronged.'

We fall silent. For a minute I don't know what to say. Then I start thinking of things to counter what she has said. Then I feel all she has said is correct and wise. 'I'm sorry. Things will be different next time,' I say lamely.

'I don't know what this abstract next time you keep talking about is, Rohan.'

149

'Next year when you are back for good. I won't force you to do any job you don't want to do. You can take all the time you want to figure out the right thing for you.'

'I'm not sure I want to come back.'

'What are you saying? Stop punishing me, Ira.'

'I'm not punishing you. It's about what will be good for me and my growth and my career.'

'So what's the answer?'

'I think I want to do a PhD. Or try for a job there.'

'But that means you'll be there for six years. Or forever. I could come there but I don't want to change my life entirely once again and then realize we can't make it work. Maybe we should spare ourselves the trouble and divorce right away.'

'There you go again!' Ira rounds on me and says. 'No, I don't want a divorce. You want a divorce because you see all these happy unions around you and feel bad that you don't have one. But marriages don't come templated, Rohan; you've got to figure out your own. You can't think of ours in terms of other people's. What worked or did not for your parents, what will or will not for Tanuj and Tanvi—these are not the same things that will hold true for us. Instead of talking about divorce, Rohan, let's talk about marriage and what it means. When I married you, I chose to experience life with you—good or bad. What marriage is it if it veers towards divorce after just a few hiccups? A marriage takes years to shape. It will happen in its own time if we look out for each other, if we help each other grow, if we make the effort to think about and act on what will help each other grow—even if it means dealing with, as in our case, the long distance.'

And with that, once again, we fall silent. In time, we reach the main market. We choose a nice Tibetan restaurant overlooking the town square and order red wine, chicken momos, pork shaphale, rice and lamb in bamboo shoot curry. And through the silence of a sour meal, only Ira's final words ring in my head: 'Instead of muddling up so many things in your head, why can't you simply be with me? Here. In the moment.'

14
Togetherness

Gangtok grows on me once I accept that it can't be what it was ten years ago. And it responds by giving us two days of only occasional spells of rain. Ira and I use the time to do touristy things. We hire a shared taxi, this time managing to get the front two seats next to the driver, to go to Nathu La, the mountain pass that connects Sikkim with Tibet. The sixty-kilometre drive takes us five hours as we move along slowly behind a long line of tourist buses, vans and cabs that wind their way uphill on the single-lane road built by the Border Roads Organization.

Even though it's cloudy and hazy, the weather is the clearest it's been in a week and Nathu La is anyway one of Sikkim's biggest attractions, our driver Sanjib tells us by way of an explanation for the swelling crowd. I discover that he worked in Mysore for some time a few years ago and knows an impressive amount of Kannada. I also get the feeling that he has taken a liking to Ira and me, because while he responds impatiently when those at the back ask him how long it will be before we reach Nathu La, he offers us extra helpings of rice and chicken curry for free when we stop for lunch at his family's restaurant on the way. So the long and somewhat uncomfortable drive does not feel all that bad.

Nathu La is teeming with more people than the number of cars prepared us for. There are sturdy honeymooning men with coy wives wearing red and white bangles up to their elbows, and there are older, less shapely couples with wailing babies—groups that I had thought the tough terrain would keep away. But, inspiringly, there are also old men and women who have braved the high altitude and low levels of oxygen just to tick a final item off their bucket lists. In the midst of these visions of what might have been our past and what could be our future are Ira and I, panting but doggedly climbing the steps to the Indian outpost at the top.

When we get there we see that the one on the other side is bigger, swankier and better maintained, with delicate Chinese motifs painted on the walls, but it is also desolate and manned by humourless soldiers. The Indian jawans reluctantly double up as travel guides and indulge the tourists' questions about Nathu La's history but absolutely refuse to let anyone take pictures, even the young women and children who think they might use their charms to get the army men to relent. So Ira and I come back down and find Sanjib, who is by now cursing our fellow passengers for taking far too long just to get a glimpse of 'the enemy'.

His short temper gets shorter on the drive back as the sky becomes overcast and his taxi starts to make sputtering sounds that he stops by and by to check. He allows us a halt of only ten minutes at Changu Lake, but it is enough to catch somebody and ask him to take a photo of us against the placid stretch of blue water. I am happy with the shot, as also with the day so far, so much so that I reinstall Facebook on my phone despite the unsteady network and immediately post the photo. My jeans pocket is abuzz with the vibration of new notifications as we reach Gangtok early in the evening. Ira ignores my juvenility. The rain starts just as we step into the hotel. And I end the day with a relaxing one hour, for the very first time, in a bathtub.

*

The next day is not so eventful or remarkable, but it is nice in a quiet sort of way. It is the day for local sightseeing, and since we are going to be in Gangtok, we decide to hire a private taxi instead of a shared one. For the rest of the day we listen to the driver's collection of hill songs and forgotten Hindi tracks from the 1990s as he drives us from the Ban Jhakri waterfall a little outside the city to the sprawling Ranka monastery and back to the Tibetology museum close to the main market.

The market is a two-hundred-metre-long and thirty-metre-wide cobbled stretch on which cars are not allowed, and on either side of which are two- or three-storey buildings painted in soft shades of green and pink. They contain restaurants, hotels and shops. The divider that runs down the middle of the road has wooden benches for tourists to take a break. It is on one of these, following an early dinner at a Nepalese home food place, that I ask Ira again if she is having a good time.

I'm hoping that her answer would have changed after the two good days, but 'I'm all right' is all she says.

'You're so hard to please,' I say. 'Tell me now where you want to go next year so I don't waste money.'

'Umm,' she says with a playful smile, 'Tokyo.'

I give her a long stare. 'Do you know everything costs like a million yens there? Tell me a place in our budget.'

'No. Tokyo,' she insists, the smile still on her face.

'Why?'

She seems to consider the question for a few seconds and then says, 'Okay, come. Let me show you.'

We walk back to our hotel, and although I am tired and want to sleep when we slip under the rajai, I agree to watch the film Ira wants us to see because it's been a while since she was so eager to share something with me. She opens her laptop and keeps it between us. It's a German film called *Kirschbluten*—cherry blossoms.

Only a few minutes into the film and I'm no longer sleepy or tired. I'm affected by the film's beauty—not breathtaking landscapes but what unfolds before us on the screen in the dark. The story is about an old, long-married couple, Trudi and Rudi, who live in a small Bavarian village. One day Trudi finds out that her husband is terminally ill, and the doctor suggests that they go on a final adventure together. She decides to keep the disease secret from him and convinces him that they should go see their children in Berlin. But when they arrive, they realize that their children are caught up in their own lives. So, from there they decide to drive to the Baltic Sea, where, even though Rudi is the one who is terminally ill, it is Trudi who suddenly dies.

I put my arm around Ira and move closer to her as Rudi stands in an empty room, curtains fluttering in the deathly quiet breeze. Rudi now discovers that he in fact barely knew Trudi at all in spite of their long marriage. He learns from his daughter's girlfriend that Trudi sacrificed her whole life for him and that her secret passions were Japan and the Japanese Butoh dance, performed in white body make-up with slow movements. And so it is that Rudi goes to Tokyo.

He visits his son who lives there, but he too wishes his father to go away. Rudi decides to make himself scarce by frequenting a park full of cherry blossoms. Here he sees a young Japanese girl who dances Butoh every day. He and the girl, Yu, soon get along because she too has recently lost a loved one, her mother, and they are able to understand each other's feelings. Trudi had often talked about wanting to see Mount Fuji. With that in mind, Rudi persuades his new friend to travel with him.

Mount Fuji is said to be so shy that it constantly hides behind clouds, so the two put up in a hotel room beside a lake as they wait for the weather to improve. Meanwhile, Rudi's delicate health starts to deteriorate. It is as if I know what is going to happen next. The mountain eludes Rudi day after day as his condition worsens. Then one night he wakes up in a fever, and as he stands outside the hotel door, the mighty Mount Fuji greets him in the bright moonshine. He wears his dead wife's clothes, puts on the Butoh make-up and starts to imitate the slow movements of the dance. Trudi then appears to him, and hand in hand they unite to create a dance before the sublime mountain. The next morning, Yu finds Rudi dead by the lake and all his savings left for her in his luggage.

I see the final scenes through a screen of tears and start crying as the film ends. Ira clearly did not expect I would react this way. She keeps asking what happened and I only repeat, 'It was so beautiful,' because in the vulnerability of the moment I don't know what else to say. I want to tell her that I've been thinking our lives are diverging, that I've been feeling sad about us drifting apart. And I want to tell her I've just realized we have this one mighty thing still left in common. But, put into words, I know it will only sound awkward.

*

I wake up the next morning feeling dead tired already in anticipation of the long drive ahead. Today we go to Lachung in North Sikkim. I know it is only about a hundred kilometres from Gangtok, but I also know that distances can be deceptive in the mountains. I remember the journey from ten years ago as a long one on undoubtedly some of the worst roads I have ever travelled on. I am up for it. I'm oddly excited by the thought of the drive. But I fear for Ira. After two good days, I think today's journey will wear her out. Worse still, I'm afraid it will really test her motion sickness. But the bookings have been done and paid for—in fact, Sharmila's contact person who confirms our excursion tells me on the phone that we are lucky we are actually able to go to Lachung as the roads were shut for two days because of a landslide and have opened just early this morning—and so we pack our bags and head to the stand from where we will be taking our shared taxi.

When we get there, we identify our ten-seater Sumo and see that others have already occupied the front and middle seats. It is a big Bengali family of six, including two children, and my heart sinks. There's no hope that the plump middle-aged uncle sitting in the front seat with his little girl will agree to switch with me and Ira. In the back are a couple, newly married, I think. And while they seem pleasant and eager to make small talk, the guy is several inches taller than me. Ira looks at me uneasily with the same thought that I have: the drive is going to be not only long but also cramped and uncomfortable. She quickly pops an Avomine.

At first I feel like I might just settle into the unsettling rhythm of the bouncy back seat. The tall guy and I quickly and silently work out an arrangement of our legs that will allow both of us to sit facing each other with the least discomfort. Our wives are falling asleep on our shoulders—holding on to, I smile as I think of it, a new gym-trained arm in my case. I close my eyes and invite sleep. But the seats are too uncomfortable for me to doze off and my bum soon becomes numb.

We halt often, sleepily step out, stretch our legs, have a cup of tea or a bag of chips, and then we resume what starts to feel like an interminable journey. The drive on the cumbersome seats and the scraggly, winding road gets worse through the day. By the time the light fades, it's killing me to remain seated. It is pitch-dark all around. I peer long and hard into this deepening gloom but fail to tell which side the mountains are on and which side the valley. Ira is up by now, but the desperation in our eyes as we stare at the road slithering endlessly ahead of us in the glare of the Sumo's headlights is so intense that we stay mum. I restrain myself from asking our driver, Bikram, how long it will be before we reach our stop for the night, because I know it's a question that annoys his kind. But I can't help but notice that we've been on the road for a little more than ten hours and there is no hint of civilization around.

The farther into oblivion we drive, the harder it becomes not to get restless. Eventually, the Bengali family succumbs. The woman by the window in the middle seat starts making clucking sounds. 'Are we close to Lachung?' she says softly to her husband in Bengali.

'Go to sleep. We will reach when we reach,' he says cockily in English from the comfort of his front seat.

The woman next to the one by the window—the two are sisters, I've had enough time to deduce that—tells the girls not to be upset. 'We will arrive soon,' she reassures them though they have not asked and have so far been rather patient and brave. It is when she tries to console them needlessly that they become whiny and start demanding good food and a warm bed.

The bug of unease spreads quickly. 'You could think of only this place?' the newly married woman diagonally opposite me curses her husband, the tall guy. I become fidgety, knowing that this is a question Ira must be trying really hard to stop herself from asking me.

Ten hours on the road become eleven and yet the end is nowhere in sight. Every turn the car takes feels like it just might be the last for the day. Every tiny light in the distance seems to hold out the possibility of emanating from our hotel. I am able to hold back the question no more and finally ask Bikram how much more time we'll take to reach Lachung. He says half an hour, and I sigh and groan and Ira has to shush me, but it turns out that Bikram was only messing with me, because we arrive at the hotel just seconds after I pose the question. He laughs as we all tumble out of the Sumo and look up mesmerized at the velvety star-spangled sky.

The hotel is not so much a hotel as a dimly lit row of rooms at the bottom of a few steps that lead down from the main road. But at least it has beds, warm blankets, hot running water and steaming rice, dal and sabzi. We wolf down the food and enter our bed without changing our clothes. There is a river flowing somewhere not far from our room. I can't see it from the window but I can hear it. And listening to the loud whistle of wind circling between two nearby mountains, I drift off to sleep.

*

We wake up at six, and when we load ourselves into our Sumo, it feels as if there was no intervening night between yesterday's time on the road and now. My body and brain are still craving rest. Ira too has overnight got dark circles under her eyes. And, by all accounts, today is going to be worse than yesterday. We are going twenty-five kilometres further north to the Yumthang Valley, from where we will retrace our tracks, have lunch at the same hotel where we stayed and then proceed downhill all the way back to Gangtok. It means yesterday's journey plus fifty kilometres on a road that is way worse than anything we have experienced so far.

Over the next two hours we realize just how far from the idea of a road a road actually can be. As day breaks, the sun lights up the desolate terrain we are in. We are slowly rolling over what is just a pathway of flattened rocks. The sight depresses me. I look sideways at Ira staring out the window.

'I'm sorry,' I whisper to her so the tall guy and his wife can't hear.

'For what?' she turns to me and says softly.

'For this holiday. You must really hate me.'

She smiles. 'Your choice of destination could have been better, yes. But I don't mind the time we are in. It'll be over soon and then we'll be sad for it.'

'*Really*?' I say. 'We've been on the road for so long and gotten nowhere. I feel bad you are here for just four months and we are wasting so much precious time.'

'And what would you rather have done with it?'

'I don't know. Something more productive than being on the road endlessly.'

Ira doesn't say anything for a while. The Sumo is silent. I look out at the road ahead through the front windshield. 'You know, that's what my thesis is going to be about next year,' Ira says to me unexpectedly.

I turn around, surprised, not just because I had thought she had dozed back off but also because it doesn't make sense. 'Your thesis? About what? Being on this road endlessly? Or this holiday?'

'No, stupid. The idea of productivity.'

'You need to explain.'

'I am going to look at artworks which question the necessity of being productive in order to present us with new ways of defining our existence.'

'Slow down, Sebastian. That's a hell of a lot of intelligent words and I don't get them.'

'I want to look at how,' she says patiently, 'when one chooses to be unproductive, one is actually asserting the innate freedom we are born with.'

'I think if I choose to be unproductive, I am asserting Maran's freedom to pack me off without severance pay.'

'That's what I want to write about.'

'*What*? About Maran and me?'

'Don't you see? Our existence is defined by our ability to be productive. We think of work as a requirement to survive, to be good citizens. But isn't it funny that those who engage in the most difficult labour and are therefore most *productive* are often the ones to be denied freedom and rights? On the other hand, unproductivity or idleness is the supreme liberty that man can hope for.'

'Are you telling me all this because you don't want to take up a job after you pass out?'

She ignores me. 'It is when you are unproductive that you can actually contemplate yourself and your capacity to act—to be productive in a way that is a true expression of your inner self. Think about it. The best creative works are products of what the rest of the world sees as long stretches of unproductive time. In the same sense, travelling is an unproductive activity but it lets you get in touch with your inner self. So is love.'

I am more serious now. 'How so?' I ask.

'Isn't it? What productive good, in the sense of the word we know, has ever come out of love? When teenagers fall in love and spend hours talking on the phone, their parents tell them to study instead. Because they feel love is a waste of time. What I want to talk about is how this wasting of time makes possible truly intimate relationships because intimacy is what is thwarted in a high-performance work culture. Intimacy is not about being together and having the same interests.' It's like she is answering all the questions I've been struggling with for a long time. 'Why else would we anguish about failing to find each other? Time *needs* to be wasted intimately. That is when you ...'

'... find love,' I complete the sentence, taking even myself by surprise. It is my turn to fall silent now. 'So when you look at it that way,' I say after a few minutes, 'this, right here—this time we are in—is not precious time wasted that could have been better spent in another way. This unproductive time is in fact productive in a truer sense as it is wasted in the interest of intimacy.'

I put it crudely but Ira does not disapprove. It makes sense now. This is why she has not, ever since she returned from New York, spoken about our fights. We are both looking at the four months we have together as some sort of trial period. But while I see it as a period in which I hope to rediscover points of convergence, she wants to know if finally, after all these years, I will learn to waste time with her intimately.

I look outside. Bikram is manoeuvring the Sumo over great inclines and through small gaps between boulders. And then, unexpectedly, I see cars parked along the pathway. We stop and disembark, and I see that the pathway too has ended abruptly.

'This is Zero Point,' Bikram declares, 'in Yumthang. This is where the road into North Sikkim ends. That mountain you see over there is in China.' It is not a point I had been to ten years ago.

Standing here in the midst of tourists in the cup of nature's palm, I can only gawp speechlessly at the white mountains that rise high above me on all sides and the tiny stream that flows by. After the long ordeal I expect Ira to be tired. But she laughs and walks off across the stream to play in the snow, beckoning me to join her. I see it for what it is. It is an invitation to waste time intimately—the closest she will come to saying that in spite of all that has happened over the past few months, she loves me still.

I order Maggi and coffee at one of the stalls. The sun is out and it's a bright morning with a cool breeze. The valley is vast and for miles there are only tall snow-covered mountains. The air buzzes with the voices of tourists, yet it feels tranquil. In that rarefied silence, I think of all that has happened in my life since Ira moved to New York nine months ago. I think of those who came into my life, held out the promise of new beginnings and left too soon. And then I think of the girl I had met on the first day of college all those years ago, who, despite the distance between us, ironically was the one who never left.

I stare at Ira walking away for a long time before joining her to play in the snow. It has been more than a week since we left Delhi, five days since we left Kolkata and four since we reached Sikkim. After a whole day's relentless journey I am now at the northern-most point in this part of the country. It has been a long, long journey into a space so remote that the inessential falls away and only the essential survives. And now I know what that is.

Ira.

15
Anniversary

This is it then. The last day of our vacation.

I usually tend to be melancholic at the end of a holiday. Not so much because the few days of relaxation, good food and pretty places to see are over. Nor so much at the thought of going back to work the next day. What makes me sad is to think I won't be able to hear my own thoughts once I return to the old mind-numbing routine.

Travel, as Ira said, lets us get in touch with our inner selves and gives us the pause to pursue what really matters. Sikkim too has been an amazing journey of self-discovery and for that I am grateful. But I am not sad the holiday is at an end. I am relieved we will at last return to Delhi, where monsoon hasn't arrived yet and whose heat and aridity I will welcome after the last four days here.

*

The rain started as a drizzle on our way back from Lachung, turning into a heavy downpour by the time we stopped for tea a while later. There we got news of a landslide at a spot we had left behind only ten minutes earlier, and of the cars which would be stuck on the road for the night. So we were fortunate in this matter and Bikram was a star. But Ira and I were not so lucky in another: the rain claimed our backpack on the carrier, leaving all our clothes soggy as mud.

Through the next day we sat in bed back in our Gangtok room staring at the dense fog, the continuing downpour and our clothes spread out on the floor to dry. When the rain let up for a short while we managed to make a quick dash to the market to buy some new clothes, but it resumed almost as soon as we were back. I called up Sharmila to ask if we could cancel Pelling, our last destination in Sikkim which was another day's journey by shared taxi from Gangtok, and instead go to Darjeeling before our flight to Delhi. But she said that the bookings were non-refundable and Darjeeling was anyway as bad as anywhere in Sikkim.

And so we are in Pelling now. We arrived late in the evening the day before and spent yesterday walking down the single winding road that makes up this quiet village. I held an umbrella over our heads—our other one was taken by the Gangtok wind—and Ira pulled it towards her whenever it veered unknowingly away.

There isn't much to do in Pelling but at least it isn't polluted or noisy like Gangtok. The guy at the reception tells me the village is so secluded that there are no shared taxis out of here. In a few hours, after a long and mostly memorable holiday, we will head back to the plains in a private car and from there fly off to Delhi. But for now I am here, it is five o'clock in the morning, I am awake as I lie in bed next to Ira and I watch her sleep.

*

Funnily, I think of Momo as I look at her. Maybe because he too has this calm, set expression when he sleeps that is reassuring. As if to say all is well with the world. Maybe he gets it from his foster mother who got him home and made sure he lived through the first few weeks of his life after we found him abandoned. I think of something Ira had said to me one day after she had moved to New York—that our children will grow up in a house with cats and dogs or any other animal they want. And suddenly it strikes me as odd. Because Ira was never fond of animals.

I have always loved animals since as far back as I can remember but Ira was different. It was most evident when she visited me and Yusuf when we lived together. She would look up recipes online and make us preparations of fish that would keep her in the kitchen for hours. And then she would get mad when she would see me siphoning off a few pieces to the cats waiting in the veranda. She would curse the cats when I let them in and they ran around the house, climbed curtains and scared her by jumping on her face while she slept at night. She was no fonder of dogs and would fearfully stay behind me as I fed the strays in JNU whenever I visited. Which is why I remember the story of how Momo came into our lives and how Ira came to love animals as odd.

It was a time when Ira and I had just got married and moved to Shahpur Jat, and happy as I was about that, I was also more than a little upset about having to leave behind the neighbourhood strays I had befriended when I lived with Yusuf. They were wild outdoor creatures who wouldn't have taken to our new third-floor flat. And though I did not say anything to Ira, she must have noticed I was moping about the separation.

Then one day, as we were returning home from our weekly vegetable shopping, we stopped on the way for momos at a Chinese cart. It belonged to a Sikkimese fellow called Sonam, whom we knew well by then since we were regulars. At first we didn't notice the pup sleeping at his feet, but when Sonam took the lid off the container to serve us momos, the tiny thing stood up and started wagging his white tail at us. Ira backed off quickly but came closer when she noticed that the pup looked too weak to attack. He was a dirty, scrawny thing, his nose encrusted with dried snot, and she dropped him a piece from her plate since he looked so malnourished.

'Do you want to take him?' Sonam asked instantly.

'What? No, no,' Ira said before I could reply.

'He toppled over the wall yesterday,' Sonam said, pointing at the fence behind him that separated Shahpur Jat from the Asian Games Village, 'and fell on my cart. All my momos fell on the ground. I kicked him but he ate up all of them. He looked so hungry that I did not have the heart to stop him. But I can't look after him.'

I wanted to take him. Shahpur Jat is full of violent stray dogs and I knew, without a home, he wouldn't live very long. I turned hopefully towards Ira, though I knew what her answer would be. But the moment I looked into her eyes, something passed between us. And I knew I wasn't imagining it—something really did. Her eyes seemed to acknowledge what was going on in my mind. I could tell she knew I wanted—*needed*—to take him home. And I could tell she knew why.

'We can't take him ...' I began to tell Sonam.

'No, we will,' Ira cut in firmly.

I looked at her. 'You don't even like animals.'

But she brushed me off again. The girl who had never been within barking distance of a dog then warily picked up the pup and we returned home, Ira cradling him in her arms. It was she who found out that he was yet too young to be fed meat and it was she who discovered we could give him a dog milk replacer. This put an end to his yelping and whimpering that kept us up in those first few nights. And once we were sure he would live, we decided to name him Momo—after his favourite delicacy.

Over the next few months Ira fell so completely in love with him and he with her that I forgot there was ever a time when she did not like animals. It is only now I remember this not unimportant detail and it makes me glad and grateful to think that she brought him home that day—agreed to share her home with a creature she knew would destroy all the furniture and upholstery she had lovingly put together for our first home—just because she thought he would make me happy.

*

I understand now. All that I have been fretting over for one year. All that caused Ira to leave me and go.

I asked myself the wrong questions and ended up with the wrong answers. I asked myself what it means to be married and the answer I got was that marriage is when two people live together and work hard to make their lives better and richer and bigger. I was so caught up in trying to live up to the answer I had got that I did not see it wasn't an answer Ira shared. I did not see I was letting her down on the promises on which we had decided to build this marriage. Even when I did ask myself the right question, I did not come up with the right answer. I asked myself what it is to love and the answer I got was that love is when two people are so like each other that they can't but be together. So when our paths diverged, I thought Ira and I had fallen out of love. In the divergence I saw a parting as inevitable. But I forgot that ours was never an orthodox love. I don't know why I tried to conform. It was never going to work for us.

But I see the truth now. I see now what Ira saw long ago. Love is not when two people are alike or when they try to be alike or when they can't bear to be away from each other. Nor is it when they decide to live together or set for themselves common life goals such as a house, a child or a retirement plan. Love is, once you are truly in its grips, a capacity for change. And once you have that figured, everything else will simply fall into place.

I drift off to sleep with the dawn of this truth, and when I wake up I see it's morning and Ira is standing at the window with her back to me. And beyond her in the distance, though we were told it hasn't been seen in a fortnight, is a cloudless view of Mount Kanchenjunga, looking every bit as resplendent as it did the first time I fell in love with it ten years ago in this very village.

'It's so beautiful,' Ira whispers to me as I join her at the window.

'Happy anniversary,' I say in response.

*

Ira looks up at me and smiles, almost as if she had forgotten what day it is. She then walks up to our backpack and comes back with an envelope in her hand.

'It was all I had money for when I left New York,' she says, handing it to me. 'Thankfully, I put it in a folder when I packed and that saved it from the rain.'

Inside, there is a simple greeting card. At its centre, stuck against a plain yellow background, is a floral-patterned robe that might be a kimono. It hangs from a stapler pin that's been made to look like a wardrobe hanger. The belt of the robe twirls around the sleeve of a man's white-and-blue-striped robe that hangs next to it from a similar stapler pin. Between them, stuck to the card, are two tiny heart-shaped beads.

I open the card. 'Dear Rohan,' it reads. 'I love you. I know I don't say it often enough. But I want you to know that I do even when I don't. Everything happens in its time. The important thing is that we look out for each other. I hope I have your back covered and you have mine. Always. Happy anniversary. Love, Ira.'

At the bottom of the card is the line: 'P.S. We'll always have each other to come back to.'

I think of the first time she had said those words to me on the night she left for New York and I smile as I see that she has finally put them down in a greeting card, as a keepsake, so that I can go back to it every time I miss her. Importantly, she has stayed true to her words.

I stare at her for a few seconds and then, overwhelmed, I engulf her in an embrace. 'After all that has happened?' I say.

'Yes,' she stares back and says. 'You never believed me when I told you before, but I did know it when we first met that we'll get married and grow old together.'

'Come on.'

'Don't believe me. But that's how it is.'

'The first time we met?'

'Yes.'

'There must have been something I did or said?'

'Not really,' she says. 'I mean, nothing extraordinary. It was the first day of college and you sat in the first row as the bell rang and everybody trooped in. I was behind you and at some point you turned around. You told me your name is Rohan and asked me for mine.'

'You remember it so well?'

'Yes,' she says.

'What did I say really?'

'You said—Ira, what a beautiful name. May this be the start of a new era.'

'And it was.'

'Yes,' she says, 'and that's when I somehow knew we'll grow old together. That we'll have a marriage that lasts the long distance—you know, the long distance of time.'

'Instead we ended up with the long distance of space.'

'That's no matter. I have a feeling we'll have time too.'

*

We are in the car now. We are driving down the beautiful mountains on a clear morning. Ira sleeps. We will go back to Delhi and some months later she will return to New York. I won't resent it this time because I know this is what makes her happy, this is what is good for her. She will not leave me this time because she wants to leave me. This time, the divergence will not be a parting of ways. If she wants to stay there, I won't ask why we are even married if we are not together. Years may go by but I know love will hold us together even when we are apart. No matter what, I know now, we will always have each other.

This marriage, this time, is for the long—and full— distance.

Acknowledgements

Life, much like this book, would be nothing without the people who shape it. For that reason I would like to express my deep, deep gratitude to:

First and foremost, Shakeel, who became Yusuf in his entirety. Thanks for being a friend, brother, best man, source of sleaze, voice of wisdom and the catcher in the rye. And for coming back for me in my Second Peloponnesian War.

Jayashree Khulge, most direct ancestor, who will remain my staunchest champion for all time to come.

My parents, Shubhada and Jagadish Inamdar, whom I will never be able to thank enough for the life they have given me.

Arcopol, dear friend during some desperate times.

Swati, for seeing merit in an anonymous submission and deciding it was worth publishing. And for helping me make it better.

Diya, for the timely, tremendous and heartfelt vote of confidence, and for championing this book along with Swati. I could not have hoped for a better publisher-editor team to work with.

Bidisha, for her careful read of the proofs.

Paru, for the lovely cover illustration, and Bonita, for translating what I had in mind on to the canvas so well, both visually and conceptually, and for the absolutely stunning final face of the book I'm proud to show the world.

Subhashree, Percy, Rahul and the entire sales and publicity teams at HarperCollins, for all the enthusiasm and help in navigating the big, bad market out there.

Sturdy pillars of support: Krishan, Shantanu and Ananth.

Trichy, Baga, Eliot, Juhu, Jeevaan, Kochi, Strip, Poker and Nemo, for all the conditional love.

Blessy, the one who never left.

Finally, Rumi, the light at the end of the long-distance tunnel, in the hope that you become Blessy. You make *every*thing worth it.